TOUCHED BY LOVE FOREVER

GIDEON O. OJO

TOUCHED BY LOVE FOREVER
This is a work of fiction. Names, character, places and incidents are either the product of author's imagination or are used fictitiously. Any resemblance to actual persons, living or dead, business establishments, events or location is entirely coincidental

Copyright © Nov., 2019
Gideon Oyedele Ojo

Watob Impact Publisher

www.watobimpact.com

watobimpact@yahoo.com

Unless otherwise stated all Scripture quotations are taken from the New International Version of the Holy Bible.

ISBN: 978-978-978-447-9

ALL RIGHTS RESERVED.

No part of this book may be reproduced in any form without permission of the Author except for brief quotations and critical reviews.

For further enquiries or information please contact:

Watob Impact LLC:

watobimpact@yahoo.com

Published in the USA

CHRISTIAN NOVEL

TOUCHED By LOVE
Forever

Gideon O. Ojo

Other books by
Gideon Ojo
- **Faith Capsule**
- **The Champion in you**

<u>Alice Abosede Ojo,</u>
You touched us with your love
which had remained indelible
in our life.

He brought me
to the banqueting house.
And His banner over me was love.
Song of Solomon 2:4

Chapter 1

> "You will show me the path of life;
> In Your presence is fullness of joy;
> At Your right hand are pleasures
> forevermore." -*Psalm 16:11*

This Sunday, the Lord's Vineyard Church Choir ministered in a way a few members of the church had not experienced before. The song they rendered was so glorious that even the 'unmoved' Louisa hummed the rhythm along with them, tapping her feet rhythmically. Louisa closely monitored the choristers in their purple robes, and the way they swerved from left to right, which made the robe look more majestic. Louisa looked at the choir mistress leading the song, who just as the rest of the choristers, repeatedly waved her hands in the air. The choir mistress was so inclined to the music that she closed her eyes shut, and she shook her head continuously to the beats, as though trying to set something loose.

Louisa expected to see the expressions and emotions of the Pastors who were adjacent to the pulpit and directly opposite the choir stand. Seated in their grey shirts, white collars, and suits, the Pastors nodded their heads, in understanding, to the songs. With his nape resting on the edge of the chair, the senior Pastor, dressed differently from the rest of the ministers in his white suit, closed his eyes meditatively and looked up intermittently, as the choristers sang their melodious song. Louisa could tell that the senior Pastor was so into the song ministration, and that his preaching that day was going to be significantly tapped from the song ministration. She looked around, and caught sight of the pastors' wives, all seated in the first pew on the right-hand side of the church; the same lane with the pastors. They all looked magnificent under their big hats. Louisa wondered why a few of them were sweating profusely, even with the ceiling fan and the air conditioner switched on and working perfectly.

Two out of the sweating lots were with their handmade fans, while others transformed their pamphlets into hand fan. Three of the Pastors' wives stood, shouting the different names of God. Louisa huffed and turned away from the sight of them, all she wanted was for them to skip to the part where donations would be made, so she could gracefully put down a tremendous amount of money. While still thinking about it, her very costly hat came off her head. She turned angrily to see who caused the fall. She frowned even more, when she saw it was a plump lady who kept on throwing her hands in the air as she let down tears. Louisa knew that no matter how much she called the lady's attention to what had happened, nothing would distract her from the worship. Louisa hissed and picked the hat, took out a handkerchief from her designer's handbag, used it to clean the hat vigorously before placing it back on her head, swearing to hit the lady if she knocked it off her head again.

The ministration stretched on and became tiring for Louisa. She folded her arms across her chest and looked directly to the altar, wishing they could just stop. At the altar, the image of Jesus Christ holding a staff and looking down at the lambs touched Louisa, almost to the point of guilt, but such feeling was far from her. Louisa was not a faithful 'churchgoer.' She attended church services just once a month, which was for thanksgiving, every first Sunday of the month. Today, just like on every first Sunday, she was there again. She got distracted at the voices of some women around her, and her gaze traveled down to them. Louisa was surprised at the scene created as the women spoke in tongues, screaming at the top of their voices. She shook her head and looked away. Louisa believed the women were merely willing to pull any kind of stunts so they could get noticed.

After what seemed like forever, the song ministration stopped, and the Senior Pastor climbed up to the pulpit that stood in between the Choir stand and the Pastors' seats, making stand facing the congregation. Looking very confident and smart, he put on a smile and then broke into a new song of worship. It uplifted the whole church once again and the already calm congregation joined him with roaring voices, leaving Louisa wondering if it was the whole of Amsterdam that came to worship with them today. She sighed as she let go of her frown; after all she was in church and could as well try to sing along, perhaps she could feel what they all felt, the spirit that moved them all. As she stood to join the congregation in worship, she noticed Veronica, her co-worker that always acted like the world was coming to an end.

Anyway, it could just be what she thought about Veronica.

Veronica held onto her hat and sang like she was not going to live the next minute if she did not sing. It annoyed Louisa, who sat back, waiting for her best moment in church services. She relaxed fully on the pew and watched people beside her render their heartfelt praises. Louisa always occupied the fifth pew on the middle row, which allowed her to be able to access people easily. She looked around even more and gave a hypercritical jeer, as she took out her mobile phone and busied herself with it.

A few minutes later, the worship died down, and the senior pastor continued his sermon. Louisa paid no attention to the pastor's sermon; she impatiently waited for him to stop his sermon. Half an hour later, the sermon was over, and it was time for tithes and donations. As the Choristers let out a chorus, people trooped out accordingly to the altar, dropping their offerings and tithes into a basket. Louisa stood up graciously, readjusted her hat, and walked out like she was on a runway. She took her time dropping her own tithe into the basket. Later, it was time for donation, and people stepped out to make their donations. After the donations, Louisa was highly appreciated for the huge amount she donated, and she beamed with a smile. After the service, Louisa left the church and marched to her car. But, she made a stop halfway when she heard her name. She recognized the voice, Veronica's.

"Good afternoon, Miss Louisa." Veronica greeted her, smiling. Louisa faked a smile.

"Good afternoon to you too, Miss Veronica." Louisa replied with a stern look.

"I hope you enjoyed the service today?" Veronica asked, still smiling.

Louisa mumbled. She didn't enjoy the entire service but enjoyed it when she was openly appreciated for the donations she made.

"Why are you leaving so soon?" Veronica asked when she wasn't getting any response to how Louisa enjoyed the service.

Louisa gave her an annoying and questioning glare.
"What do you mean?"

"Oh, I mean, are you not waiting for the fellowship of the single sisters." Veronica asked.

Louisa let out a wry laugh. Veronica must have thought Louisa was desperate to get married just like she was.

"I have work to do, unlike you. I have many companies and people to market my products to." Louisa replied harshly.
Veronica smiled, "I understand you are busy, but it is just for one hour."

"One hour? That is enough for you to lose two valuable customers and buyers. Now I understand why you never make any sales. Besides, are you not supposed to be at work today?" Louisa replied. She saw the expression on Veronica's face. This statement must have hit Veronica hard. Her smiles faded slowly.

"I give my time to God, and I believe I do my work just fine." Veronica replied.

Louisa smirked. She knew Veronica just said what she did so as not to lose the battle of words. Veronica smiled again, and this time, it spread across her face. Louisa was taken aback, but she was not going to wonder why Veronica was smiling. She has no time for people with less importance in her life.

"It would be nice if you joined us. You are always welcome whenever you are ready. Now, if you would excuse me." Veronica said, and walked away.

Louisa watched her walk away. She wondered what gave her the nerve to talk to her that way. Louisa was Veronica's senior colleague after all; she should acknowledge her with a little respect. Louisa hissed and walked to her car that was not too far away. She got in and drove off.

> "But the ones that fell on the good ground are those who, having heard the word with a noble and good heart, keep it and bear fruit with patience." -*Luke 8:15*

Veronica got home some minutes past 2' o clock. She was exhausted, and lazily dropped her handbag on the floor, slumping on the chair that was closer to the entrance of her apartment. She kicked off her shoes and sighed heavily, staring at the wall clock in front of her. She has less than an hour to be at the office. Then, she heard some sound coming from the kitchen. She looked at her house keys in her hands, suddenly realizing that she had not opened the door with the keys; it was opened already. She stood up abruptly, walked slowly to the door and picked the umbrella behind the door. She began reciting Psalm 23, as she gradually approached the kitchen with the umbrella in her hands, ready to use it on whoever it was.

"The Lord is my shepherd; I shall not want. He makes me to lie down in green pastures; He leads me beside the still waters. He restores my soul; He leads me in the paths of righteousness for His name's sake. Yea, though I walk through the valley of the shadow of death, I will fear no evil; for you are with me; your rod and your staff, they comfort me... Mum!" She yelled when she saw that the intruder was her mother.
She dropped the umbrella.

"Hello, love." Her mother greeted her, coming out from the kitchen. Veronica's eyes followed her mother.
"But Mum, what are you doing here? And how did you get in?" Veronica asked as she followed her mother, who was settling down in the living room. Her mother picked her scattered shoes and bags from the floor.

"Mum!"
"Fine, I came to cook for you. I know how tired you get on Sundays and I got your spare keys from Ann." her mother confessed.

Veronica grunted. She had explicitly made it clear to her sister not to give their mother her spare key, and now this is what she gets in return, betrayal. Veronica looked at her Mother's eyes; they were old, and the skin surrounding the eyes was full of wrinkles. Even her once-upon-a-time blonde hair was partly grey. She knew her mother meant well, but she was just not ready for whatever her mother had in stock for her this afternoon.

"Happy Sunday, Mum." she finally greeted her mother with a peck on the cheeks. Veronica collected her shoes and bags from her.

"A married woman would never leave the house disarrayed and scattered. What if your children injure themselves when they play with your heels that you left carelessly on the floor?" Her mother questioned.

Veronica rolled her eyeballs. "Mum, I don't have a child, talk less of children, plus I'm not married." she said as she walked into her room. Her mother followed her.

"Well, don't you plan to get married someday and have kids?"

Veronica sighed; she knew this conversation was going to go on for a while. She dropped her shoes in her closet and joined her mother on the bed, where she had settled for the extended discussion.

"Mum, someday. Not today, not tomorrow."
"I hope it is soon."

"Patience, Mum. Patience is everything." Veronica said and held her mother's hand. They were cold; she rubbed her hands against her mother's.

"You have been saying this patience word for years now. Veronica love, you are thirty-two years old. You are getting old. Very soon, men won't look your way anymore." her mother said with a bothersome tone.
Veronica nodded.

"Mum, Romans 5 verses 4 says, ... and patience, experience; experience, hope."
Her mother looked away, but she pulled her mother's chin, so she could look at her directly in the eyes.

"Mum, the world may be broken, but the hope is not crazy. We have to be patient and hopeful in God. He doesn't fail his own, okay?"

Her mother nodded and hugged her tightly. She had her worries; Veronica was still single and was not even in a relationship. She really hoped that hope is not crazy in this sense. Veronica slowly pulled away.

"If you keep on holding onto me, I think my spouse is not the only thing we would be looking up to God for. Opportunity for a new job would be added to the list." she said, and her mother gave her a confused look.

"Mum, I have to be at work by 3pm. I'm running late already."
Veronica laughed, and her mother joined her, too, when she finally understood the comic in her statement.

"Okay. I'll go and continue cooking while you dress up for work." Her mother stood up from the bed, walked to the door and stopped. "You know I love you, regardless of anything." she said with all sincerity and gave an intentional weird look.

Veronica understood what it meant.
    "Mum! I'm not a lesbian."
She laughed.
    "If you say so," her mother said mockingly.

"I say so because I know so. Just leave, so I can dress up and leave for work before you render me jobless." Veronica said and went to the door. As soon as her mother left, she closed the door behind her. Veronica can't blame her mother for thinking she was a lesbian. She knew her mother had every right to feel that way. Ever since Veronica hit puberty, she has never introduced any boy to her mother as a boyfriend or someone she loves. Veronica had crushes on different guys and had her own shares of dishonest men that have left her heart broken so many times. Veronica had finally concluded after the last heartbreak not to go into a relationship until she has met the right man God has assigned to her.

She took off her Sunday outfit and changed into a corporate wear. She packed her blonde hair in ponytails and stood in front of her mirror. Standing in front of her mirror made her see a clear reflection of herself; she was not getting any younger. She didn't look as beautiful as she did some years back. Her green eyes were almost looking faded. She was now chubby and looking older than thirty-two. She wondered what was weighing her down. She sighed, deciding not to look at herself in the mirror once more. She did not want to worry about how she looked. Seeing her hair in ponytail reminded her of Kwame. He likes her hair down, like a flowing river. Kwame was someone she admired and loved very much back in high school. He was her high school sweetheart, and back then, she would have very much liked to be with him. They were friends for a while, and she knew him to be a flirt with ladies. So, when he asked her to be his girlfriend, she refused. In a bid to avoid constant pain and heartbreak, not knowing many of such awaited her in the nearest future. Although Veronica blamed herself a lot for rejecting him, she was still thankful that she did. She smiled, just at the thought of him and hoped that wherever he was, he was doing fine with his charming and seductive smile.

"Veronica! You are going to be late if you don't come out of your room now." yelled her mother.
Veronica jerked up from her memory lane.

"Coming!" She said, and hurriedly packed her bag, putting her car keys, personal laptop and wallet in her bag.

Chapter 2

> "But seek ye first the kingdom of God and His righteousness, and all these things shall be added unto you." -*Matthew 6:33*

Early on Monday morning, Louisa walked elegantly into the company. Her heels did an excellent job of creating awareness about her presence. She was on a high waist, autumn belted trousers and a white chiffon top imprinted with red polka dots. The cape fell over her shoulders to her back. Her brunette hair was in wavy form, and she let it fall down her back, resting on the cape. She purposely left a smile on as she walked past her co-workers. Louisa wanted them to feel the confidence she has in herself, and made sure they got the message that she did not care about what anyone had to say about her. Finally, she got to her office, which she shared with other marketers. The marketing department was a bit competitive when she just joined, and she knew how hard she had toiled to get to where she is now. The marketers have all lost their styles and marketing sense. Louisa had barely sat down at her desk when a messenger delivered coffee and bagel to her. That was how she liked it; she didn't need to remind anybody about anything.

One of the marketers, Lillian, who had become Louisa's personal assistant over the years, walked smartly to her, to feed her of the day's business.

"Good morning, Miss Louisa." Lillian greeted smiling.
Louisa slowly dropped her cup of coffee, and Lillian followed the cup's motion until she noticed that Louisa's lipstick had stained the cup. Good thing, it was a disposable cup Lillian thought. She knew nobody would like to share a cup with Louisa, primarily because of the venom that spewed out of her.

"What?" Louisa roared.
Lillian trembled at the roar.
"I just came to feed you on the day's detail ma."
Louisa frowned. Lillian always had a way of stepping on her toes every day, and she didn't know if she could take it anymore.

"I believe you are not blind, Lillian! Can't you see I'm busy, or do you plan with the others to evict me from my seat by choking me to death?"

"I'm sorry ma. It is just that we have a meeting with the board and the production team by nine concerning the new skincare product that is on the ground." Lillian said in fear of what Louisa could do to her for not giving her the information beforehand.

Louisa looked at the wall clock in the office, a few minutes before eight. She heaved a sigh.

"Honestly, I don't know what to do to you. You are so dumb. How can you just tell me of a meeting we have by nine at this time? And you confidently stand before me to talk. You are not going to ruin my reputation in this company."

Louisa stood up from her chair, and Lillian stepped back a little, heads bowed to the floor. She dared not look eye to eye at Louisa.

"Get the hell out of my way." Louisa said and pushed Lillian out of her way. She walked out of the office and headed straight for the office of the chief of production. They had a deal that he would always inform her beforehand about new products so that she could plan her marketing strategies on time, but he didn't keep to his own end of the deal. Well, Louisa was going to give him a piece of her mind before the meeting. She stormed angrily into his office, ignoring people's greeting and his secretary's caution that she couldn't go in.

When she got into the office, a lady dressed in a tight-fitted skimpy gown was with him, and from the way they had hurried back to their supposed normal position, she could tell that something was going on before she barged in. Louisa cared less anyways.

"Louisa!" Mr. Lockwood called her name, mostly in shock.

She saw the look of guilt on his face, but it disgusted her. She held back the words that were about to come out from her mouth. She stood akimbo and shot his visitor a poisonous look. Perhaps the look sent the right message to his visitor, or she was just tactful enough to know she had to leave them alone, she hurriedly packed her bag and stood up to leave.

"Goodbye, Mr. Lockwood. I'll see you around." she said and left but not without returning Louisa's poisonous look. Louisa and Mr. Lockwood were both silent for a few minutes afterward. Louisa watched him stand up from his chair to readjust his tie and his belt. He took his white lab coat from the single hanger in the room and wore it.

"Louisa, if you really don't have anything to say, I would have to leave you in this office because I have a brief meeting with my team members before the meeting with the board and your department today." he said as he comfortably sat back on his chair.

Louisa scoffed, and for some moment, her attention was drawn to the poster of a plant on his wall; the plant was so green, and her brain did a brief thinking. Everything was a lie. Their company made no natural or organic skin care products, although that was what they were known for. Their products were all from chemicals. Like a flash of lightning, she remembered why she was in his office.

"Mr. Lockwood, we had a deal. I kept to my own end of the deal, but you didn't. What would it have taken you to put a call through to me? I mean, I just found out that there is a new product." she growled.

He gave a crooked smile.

"Oh! Louisa. My sweet Louisa. When last have you treated me good? I mean, I haven't gotten down there in months." he said, positioning his eyes in between her legs. Louisa held her head high.

"Lady, it's been three months now, and you expect me to run around like your puppet and tell you every information that comes my way? Wake up, girl! This is business."

"I see. You have no shame." Louisa said in disgust.

He laughed and stood up from his chair. He came closer to Louisa, and then pulled her to sit on the chair, which the previous lady formerly occupied. Louisa was vexed. If he thought he was going to bring her so low, and take her for a cheap whore, he was wrong. She pushed his hands away from her body, stood up, and looked him in the eyes.

"Go buy yourself a bit of dignity. It would help you well." She gritted her teeth.

"It's funny. A kettle calling the pot black."
"We are the same, love. We do not differ in any way." She looked at him sternly.

"Don't you sleep with your clients to market the products and have them buy it?" He said with no caution. Louisa chuckled and walked out of his office, slamming the door really hard.

The meeting started at precisely nine and ended a few minutes past eleven. Mr. Lockwood did his best to spite Louisa throughout the meeting. It pissed Louisa off, but she had to be calm and relaxed. Louisa knew his actions would definitely arouse suspicions and that was why the weird looks Louisa got from people didn't surprise her. As she headed to her office after the meeting, she saw her co-workers in groups having chitchats and whenever they saw her coming, they would make queer faces. Their gossip about her is the least they could do to hurt her, she basically didn't care what they thought or said about her. Everything is fair when it comes to business. She raised her head up and walked more graciously, taking her time to move one step after the other.

"Miss Louisa, would you like to go in your car or the company's car?" Lillian asked.

Louisa, who had her head buried in her laptop, looked up at Lillian. It took a few seconds for her to understand why Lillian would ask such a question.

"How many marketers are going out this morning?" Louisa asked.

"Just three marketers. Yourself, Mrs. Andrea, and Miss Veronica."

"Veronica?"
Lillian nodded.

Louisa doesn't want anything to do with Veronica. It was enough that church services and the office brought them together, but she would very much love to avoid her as often as she could. Veronica's sad baggy eyes were something she didn't want to have to look at, under any circumstances.

"They can go without me. I will go in my own car later, maybe in the afternoon." Louisa said, concentrating on her laptop.

"Okay ma. I will let them know you are not coming with them."

"Since when do you report my movements to them." Louisa said fiercely.

Lillian short of words; she had never done that before, but saying anything to justify herself now would only make the issue worse. She shook her head and looked down.

"Get out of here." Louisa barked.

Everybody was getting on her nerves today, and it was annoying. Louisa felt the need to receive fresh air and a cool breeze, something to make her calm down. She picked her mobile phone and exited the office, got into the elevator and stopped at the rooftop. Louisa stood very close to the edge of the railings; inhaled fresh air and closed her eyes. At that moment, she wished everyone could disappear and it would be just her in the world, with a lot of money to spend. Louisa felt at ease, and the world seemed peaceful. She opened are eyes and exhaled, but everything was still the same. The numerous skyscrapers all over the city were still there, the bustling sounds of vehicles were still loud enough, even the birds chirped about, and the flowers-decorated rooftop didn't change a bit. She sighed.

> **"Commit your way to the Lord; Trust also in Him, And He shall bring it to pass."** -*Psalm 37:5*

As Veronica sighted the old grey porch, she recalled having friends come over to talk about their wedding days and how glorious it was going to be. Most of her friends were married already, and just a few of them were left. Veronica rang the doorbell once and waited patiently for the door to be opened by someone. She hoped it would be her ever smiling and encouraging sister, Maureen.

"Look who is finally here!" Janet, her immediate sister announced the moment she saw Veronica.

"Aunt Vero!" Maureen's six years old twins echoed as they ran to her. They jumped on Veronica, who really did not have the strength to carry them at once. She converted it to an embrace as she stooped down to their height.

"Guess what I got for you?" Veronica asked, excited to surprise them.

They both exchanged a glance and smiled, and then they turned to Veronica with a knowing smile.

"Gummy bears!"

"No, chocolates!" She said, feeling defeated.

"Yeah!" They chorused again, and reached for her handbag. She let them have it; Veronica smiled as she watched them run into the living room. She took off her coat, but when she saw that the coat hanger was occupied already, she knew they were all present. She hung her jacket on one of the coats and walked to the living room. It smelled really lovely in there, and it felt like Christmas. The picture frame of her family members and herself hung all over the walls. She smiled at the sight of her ten year-old self.

"Remind me to never leave my kids with you for more than a day." Maureen said as she came into the living room. She was heavily pregnant, expecting her next child.

"Maureen, how are you?" Veronica asked, hugging her sister, doing her possible best not to hold her too tight because of the baby.

"Aunt Vero, hi." Jake, Janet's eight year-old son greeted plainly. He was never one for too much drama.
"Jacob, come here. Come give your aunt a warm hug. She needs it." Veronica said sweetly. He was reluctant at first, but he had no choice, so he went to her and hugged her.

"Hello, Vero." Tom, Maureen's husband greeted Veronica as she stepped into the dining room. He was busy setting the table.

"Hey." Veronica said, and patted his back.
"Mum, I'm here!" Veronica called her mother, who was in the kitchen.

"And you are late." Her mother responded.
Veronica saw that coming, so she smiled and joined her mother in the kitchen. Maureen was with her.

"I'm sorry. I was occupied with work." Veronica apologized, hugging her mother from behind.

"You are not going to get married to work now, are you?"
Veronica slowly let go. Her mother was so good at hitting the nail on the head.

"Even those with families got here earlier, and I know they work to feed their families." Her mother added.
"Momma!" Maureen called in a shrilled voice, turned to her sister, and smiled.

"Pay no attention to mum, she's been cranky all day." Maureen whispered to Veronica, loud enough for their mother to hear her.

> **Remember now your Creator in the days of your youth, Before the difficult days come, And the years draw near when you say, "I have no pleasure in them"**: -*Eccl. 12:1*

They sat down in silence for dinner. Veronica ate slowly. She used her fork to play around with the carrot and pickles in her plates. Maureen kept on giving her encouraging smiles, but they did little to help uplift her burdened heart.

"Why are you slow to eat? Do you have a dinner date tonight?" Janet asked.

They all went silent on the table, even the children. Veronica looked up from her plate and looked at everyone. Her mother's eyes carried a glimmer of hope; Veronica knew that deep down, her mother wished for a definite answer. Veronica shook her head.

"No." She said plainly.

"No? And you gave us all a minute of suspense." Janet blurted.

Veronica looked at Janet.

"I barely have time for that. I have church activities to meet up with."

"Yea, right church activities." Janet said with a mocking note on 'church activities.' "Holier than thou." Janet added.

"I heard that." Veronica said.

"So?"

"Janet!" Maureen called her to caution. "Be mindful of what you say."

Janet scoffed. "Isn't that what you do best? You take her sides always. What's so wrong in what I've said? Huh? Mother?" She said and turned to her mother.

Her mother looked away. Janet felt betrayed, and it hurt her whenever no one took sides with her.

"Family is overrated. You, Veronica, were the one who castigated me and criticized me when I got pregnant out of wedlock. You were holy then, weren't you? Well, I see the man your Christianity has gotten you." Jane ranted in pain and anguish.

"Janet, you do realize that is not the situation here. That is in the past." Veronica shouted.

"Girls!" Their mother called, but they were too heated to hear her. Maureen ushered the kids away from the dining room.

"It has always been about that, and it was never in the past. Do you think I'm going to show you pity because you are passing through a phase? You never did show me pity. You scolded me all the way."

"Janet! That's enough!" Their mother hit the table hard.
Veronica was almost at the brink of tears now. She stood up, and all she could see was the hatred and fury from her sister.

"Janet, I am your big sister." Veronica said and sniffed, trying to hold down the tears. "I love you, and I would do anything to make you happy." She used her hands to wipe the tears that were rolling down her eyes. "But I would never ever go blind when you ought to be corrected and chastised for your wrongdoing. That is who I am." She looked away from her sister, wiped her tears again, and continued. "And, I am sorry if I went too far, it was all out of love. I am really sorry." She pushed her chair backward and made to exit the house.

"Veronica!" Her mother called.
Veronica stopped and turned to Janet.

"Mind you, I am not in any phase. God's will is supreme, and He is the one I lean on and trust, not men or family." She said this and stormed away. So much for family dinner, she thought.

Chapter 3

> "Behold, at that time I will deal with
> all who afflict you; I will save the lame,
> and gather those who were driven out;
> I will appoint them for praise and fame.
> in every land where they were put
> to shame." - *Zephaniah 3:19*

Veronica got late to Church for the evening service, which made her sit at the back pew. She so much despised being late and sitting at the back, but she had no choice. The message was ongoing; she made a brief prayer and quickly concentrated on the message.

"As a Christian, how many times have you donated money to the orphans? Have you ever given alms to the needy? We see the handicaps everyday of our lives, but what have we done to help them? I say to you today, contribute to the lives of people in need; the handicaps that need assistance, and become their aid. Volunteer to help them, you don't have to be forced to do something for them; neither do you need someone to tell you what you ought to do to help; but your heart, when in the right alignment with God should tell you what to do. Leviticus 19:14 says, 'You shall not curse the deaf or put a stumbling block before the blind, but you shall fear your God: I am the LORD." the Pastor said, took out a handkerchief and wiped the sweat from his forehead before continuing

"Also, the book of Galatians chapter 6 verse 2 says, 'Bear one another's burdens, and so fulfill the law of Christ.' Therefore, brethren in Christ Jesus, I beseech you this week, go and help the needy, give alms, volunteer in homes, assist the poor. In any way you can help; help so that you can glorify our Father in Heaven. Let's bow our heads to pray." instructed the Pastor, and they all bowed their heads silently to pray.

Veronica was moved by the message, and it touched her heart deeply, so much that she decided to register as a volunteer the following day and to be dedicated to it. Never for once as it ever crossed her mind to do so, but now that the message had come to her, she would not forsake it.

Veronica got home to meet her mother and Maureen outside, waiting for her. Maureen was smiling widely as she spread her arms broadly to hug her sister. Veronica smiled and hugged her. She went to her mother and did the same.

"Hi, Mum."
Her mother pecked her cheeks.
"What are you guys doing here? It's late and cold, come in." Veronica said as she opened the door.

They stepped in one after the other. Maureen sat down on one of the cushions and quickly massaged her leg.

"Mum, I thought you had the spare key to my house. Why didn't you enter earlier?" Veronica asked, dropping her bag and taking off her coat.

"I know, but I want to respect your privacy. "Her mother said grinning as she also settled down beside Maureen.

"That's so sweet, Mum, but not at the expense of you freezing up my baby niece." She said, pointing to Maureen's stomach. Maureen laughed.

"Hey, not fair! What about the mother?" Maureen asked, laughing.

"Well, I think she's doing just fine." She replied and sat down on the chair opposite Maureen's.

"Anyway, how was work today?" Maureen asked.
"Fine."

"And Church?" Her mother added.
Veronica looked at her mother, suspiciously. "Fine."
There was a bit of an awkward silence. Veronica looked at both of them as they exchanged glances. She caught Maureen giving their mother a 'go-ahead' look.

"Veronica, I really don't want to beat about the bush; so, are you free on Friday night?" Her mother asked. Veronica could guess why her mother would ask such a question.

"I hope I'm not." She replied, with no interest.

"Come on! I got a blind date for you with...." Veronica was sure her mother still had a lot to say but, she was not in the mood to hear any of it.

"Mum, please. I thought we are over that. We agreed I wasn't going to meet my future husband through a blind date. God will bring him to me directly." Veronica explained calmly.

"Ve-ro, I looked through his profile, he's a good catch. He's rich and so handsome, no back story, just a normal guy, searching for his bride." Maureen chipped in.

"Really? Maureen, not you too. Please, I have no time for blind dates and the likes. I have Jesus to concentrate on, and Mum, I think you should trust in Jesus too. You want me to get married so badly? Please pray for me rather than arranging blind dates."

"Veronica, I have tried, really. What else can a mother do for her child? Why are you making such a big deal out of everything?"

"This is not me making a big deal out of anything, okay? I'm just trying to be realistic." Veronica replied to her mother.

"Are you saying I am living in a fantasy? How dare you!" Her mother was getting angry at her, and that was the last thing Veronica wanted from her mother right now. Maureen dived in to ease the tension their mother was already having. "Momma, I am sure that's not what Vero meant. Just calm down, okay? We can only suggest, but she decides. It is her life after all."

"Thank you, Maureen. Mum, if I am chanced on Friday night, I will go on a date. Is that okay?"
A bright smile spread across her mother's face; she nodded.

"Is that all? Is there something else you have to tell me? I mean, you came all the way here to tell me something, right?" Veronica looked from her mother to her sister. The blank look on their faces confirmed the answer she suspected.

"That's all we came to tell you." Her mother replied.
"Seriously?"
"We also came to check on you." Maureen added.

Veronica laughed, Maureen joined her, and their mother followed suit. She felt at ease, a moment to smile with family, a moment to escape thoughts and worries.

After a while, they left for their various homes. Veronica was glad Maureen came to this world as her sister. Maureen had always been a shoulder she can rest on from time to time, She understood her better than anyone else. Janet had always opposed her in everything they do. Right from when they were kids, they had never for once stood on the same side. It hurt Veronica a lot that things still remained the same after so many years. Even when Janet got pregnant, she never really understood Veronica's point of view that everything she said and did was purely out of love. Veronica sighed as the thought of her sister flooded her mind. She took out her mobile phone and dialed Janet's number, but it went into voicemail. She recorded a brief message asking after her well-being. Family is essential, and she loved every one of her family, even her father, regardless of his misdeeds back in the days.

Veronica's father had never taken any of them seriously, not even their mother. If he was not out getting drunk, he was in jail for one crime or the other. Prison became a home to him. Somehow, his wife, Veronica's mother didn't know how or why, but she always forgave him, and still loved him even after his death. His death was something no one in the household talked about because of the shame it brought to their family name.

Veronica took longer than usual in the shower tonight. She was filled with thoughts of her family members. The moment she got out of the bathroom, she took out her mobile phone and went on the internet, registered as a volunteer in a home that called Happy Home. Dressed in her nightgown, she took her Bible and laid on her bed.

> "Flee sexual immorality. Every sin that a man does is outside the body, but he who commits sexual immorality sins against his own body." -1 Corinthians 6:18

Louisa did not feel enthusiastic as she always felt whenever she was going out to market products. All she wanted to do that day was to sit behind her desk lazily all day long, but it was out of option for her. She was lagging behind in sales, and that was something she didn't tolerate. It was almost a week since the product was out for marketing and she had made only two sales to companies she couldn't wholly rely on. With an energized mind, she stood up, packed her bag, and cleared her table. She called for Lillian and asked for the list Lillian had compiled for her on the warehouses to which she could market the products. They all looked like a good catch, but she was going for the fourth one on the list, C. T Wholesales & Co.

"I'll just market in one place today, and tomorrow I'll go for the rest." She said and returned the list to Lillian.

"Okay ma, you are the best!" Lillian said.
Louisa looked at her scornfully. Although she liked to be praised, she just didn't feel like it this afternoon. She walked out of the office, hopped into her car, and drove straight to Hooftstraat Street.

When she got to C.T Wholesales and Co, she had to wait for thirty minutes before she could see the CEO, who appeared to be the Product Manager also. Waiting wasn't something Louisa appreciated, but she had picked this place out for the day. The waiting room was calm and quiet; it was just her and the receptionist there. They exchanged weird stares. At first, Louisa had not taken notice of the way the lady receptionist gawked at her. Instead, she was occupied looking at all the paintings of Jesus Christ and the posters of Bible quotes. It was more than the ones she had to look at in church. What is this place? She wondered. Louisa was still busy glaring when her gaze finally fell on the receptionist, and she caught the receptionist giving her those looks she often get from "holy ladies." Louisa returned the looks, and it was even worse.

After the receptionist received a call from who Louisa guessed to be the boss, thanks to her constant 'yes sir,' she ushered Louisa into his office. Louisa adjusted her skirt by pulling it up to make it look shorter than it should be; she wanted this meeting to go fast. She walked into the office like a sly pussycat.

The office was large, with three large armchairs positioned at a corner and a table at the center. Louisa smirked with the thought that they can do it quickly on the chair if he wanted it that way. She looked away from the chairs and then to the 5 feet tall figure by a shelf, with sleeves rolled up, holding a book and smiling at her.

His smiles were beautiful, which made her wobble a little, but he rushed to her and helped her gain her balance. While he searched for what could cause her sudden stumble, she took the liberty to assess him accurately. His first two buttons were undone, and it revealed a little bit of his brown skin chest, which she guessed was broad enough. His hair was so curly that she badly wanted to put her hands through them to straighten it.

"Sorry about that. Sit down, let me get you water." He said and broke into her assessment.

Louisa gave a seductive nod and devious smile. He took a glass from his drawer that was next to his shelf, went to his water jug, and poured in a full cup. He stretched it out to Louisa, who was still staring at him awkwardly, intentionally;

she touched his fingers that held the glass as she received it from him.

He returned to his seat across Louisa, and watched her as her hazel eyes never turned away from his, even as she drank the glass of water.

"I guess you are good now?" He asked as she dropped the cup on the cup mat he had earlier dropped on the table.
"Yes."

"Okay. Miss Louisa, from Evergreen Skincare and Cosmetic Company. It's an honor to meet you." He called her name from a card before him.

"Thank you, Mr. Turner."
He nodded. Louisa looked above his head, to the wall. There was a Bible verse there, it reads: "Do not overwork to be rich; Because of your own understanding, cease!" Proverbs 23:4

"So, what do you have for me?" He asked her. She lifted the bags that carried the products and dropped them on the table.

"This is our latest product in Evergreen Skincare and Cosmetic Company. It is 100% organic, and it comes with a lot of benefits for the skin. Finally, we have gotten a solution to rough skins; it has been guaranteed that within two weeks of use, the skin changes for the better." She paused, and then looked at him. He was paying close attention to her, and attention is what pleased her. He reached out for one of the parcels.

"It looks really promising, but what do I gain from being a wholesaler to your Company. What are my profits?" He said and relaxed on his chair.

Louisa smiled. This was the part where she played her role; this was the same question all other wholesalers and buyers asked that she took advantage of to pin them down. She stood up, ran her hand through her hair, and slowly walked over to him.

"You have a lot to gain aside from the money; you have the whole of me and my body to gain at your beck and call." She said as she placed her hands on his chest.

He stood up and looked at her with so much disgust, trying his best to hide the ongoing emotions, but he couldn't. She appalled him.

"Does this work for every of your client? I mean to say every person you market to? I won't pretend to know what you are up to, so I will just tell you straight. I can't, and I won't buy your products if this is the way you market and sell it alongside with your body."

That was a surprise counter back.
"What?!" She said alarmed.
"Yes. I'm afraid, Miss Louisa but, I have to ask you to leave my office now. I have some business to attend to." He said and pointed to the door.

"What are you talking about?" She asked mainly because she was surprised that he turned her down at the first attempt. No one has ever turned her down; she was a vixen in this deal, why was he turning her down?

"Miss Louisa, seduction isn't one of the keys to selling your products, if you must know. If you have been doing it before, I'll have to tell you to stop it."

"Huh? Oh, I see." She said and smile. "You don't want to do it here, right? You can pick any hotel you want, and we'll get over with it." She continued holding his bare hands.
He took her hands off him.

"Your body is the temple of Christ; don't you know that?" He continued when he saw she had a blank expression on her face. "Miss Louisa, look, there are things we do to acquire wealth, but not through devious means. True wealth comes from God alone, and not like this."

Louisa could have sworn she saw ten thousand people mocking her, she felt rejected and mostly angry. How dare him?

"Whatever. Save your preaching for your family, I am not one of them. This is business, that's how we roll. So you can keep your damn money to your pocket, Mr. Turner. Goodbye." Louisa spoke in frustration. She picked her bags as she stormed out of his office.

Who was he to think he can put her off like that, and then bring the Bible into the whole situation? He could have said he was not interested and that was all, what gave him the guts to talk to her like she was some filthy rag. His wholesales company was not even that big. It would not cost her Company anything if they lost deals with C.T Wholesales. She hit her steering wheel as she drove. Veronica should have come to him; that way, they would have a prayer session together.

Louisa drove home straight. She felt too much rage to go back to work. She flung her bag on the floor as she got home, and paced about for almost twenty minutes, with no particular thoughts, just rage, and anger. She had never felt so dirty, worthless, and useless in her life. Ever since she started sleeping with men to market her goods for years now, no one had ever made her feel this way. She pulled her hair as she remembered the looks in his eyes, he was disgusted at the sight of her.

"Arhhhhh!" Louisa screamed.

How could he confidently turn her down and still feel no remorse, he was so cool about it. He had the effrontery to give her Bible talks.

She walked to her bathroom, turned on the shower, and stepped into the bathtub, which was directly under the shower, with her clothes on. Louisa wanted to wash away that feeling of dirt Mr. Turner made her feel. She took off her clothes one after the other, poured all her soap on herself, sponged her body really hard, but it still won't go. She cried!

Louisa could not remember the last time she wept over something or anybody, but now she was feeling so low, she thought she had been dragged to the mud and marched over countlessly. After an hour, she came out of the bathroom, fell to her bed, and slept off.

> "But I say to you that whoever divorces his wife for any reason except sexual immorality causes her to commit adultery; and whoever marries a woman who is divorced commits adultery." -*Matthew 5:32*

Louisa found herself in a very familiar environment, an old one. The one which has been buried deep in her memory. She saw herself, that cute eight year old that she was, the one that grew up to forget what it felt like to be loved and cherished. She looked around only to discover she was in her old room, the room she stayed before her parents got divorced. Her favorite bunnies lied quietly on her bed as they watched her eight-year-old self, listening to her parent's heated conversation.

"Nick! I swear to God, I am so tired of your broke ass that I can't even stand the sight of you anymore." Her mother yelled at her father.

Louisa watched her herself open the door and step out, she followed suit.

"You don't like my broke ass; I don't like your slutty attitude." Her father replied.

"Oh, please, everyone knows you are the one who goes about having sex with bitches and sluts with the little money you make. You should be ashamed of yourself. I mean, you have a daughter, and what do you expect her to think of you?"

"That's if she's my daughter."

"Nick, are you crazy? Have you lost your mind? She's your daughter, our daughter."

"Yeah?"

"Yeah. You know what? I can't believe you right now. Go find money because I've prepared divorce papers for you. I'm divorcing your raggedly broke self; nobody wants to die in poverty. Go get ready." Her mother said.

Little Louisa never wanted her parents to get separated. She had always wished for them to come to an agreement for once, but that had never happened, and she didn't think it ever will.

"Divorce? Oh, hell yeah. That's exactly what I want."

"Mummy! Daddy! You are not getting a divorce, are you?" Little Louisa asked.

"Girl, get out of here. What are you doing out here? You should be in bed now." Her mother scolded.

Little Louisa looked at her father, then her mother. She held her mother.

"Mum, please. Don't divorce dad, things are going to get better, right dad?"

Her mother released her hands from Louisa's grip. It was so violent that it made Louisa fall to the ground. She cried as she fell and her father picked her up.

"Baby, everything is for the best, okay? Go to bed." He pacified her and dropped her.

Louisa watched herself sniff as she walked sadly to her bedroom, with the knowledge that all hopes about her parents were gone.

Suddenly, Louisa felt a massive wind blow her, and in a twinkle of an eye, she met herself in her teenage home, where she lived with her mother and her rich stepfather. She tried screaming to get out of there, but her voice was gone. She pushed an unfamiliar door; it led her to the room she occupied in the house. Her seventeen-year-old self came into the room with a heavy heart. Her mother stormed in angrily.

"Look here, whore. I won't let you look at my husband with those seducing eyes of yours. You want to be a harlot? Go to the brothel. Make your slut money there and not from my husband." Her mother warned her.
"Ma, you can't talk to me like that." She spoke back at her mother.
Her mother slapped her.

"I can talk to you the way I want, and there is nothing anybody can do about it, not even your dumb father."

"That you married and once loved." Louisa yelled back in tears. "If I can recall, you are the harlot. You stole someone else's husband when you were barely out of your divorce case. You should be ashamed to call yourself a woman." The teenage Louisa spat out.

Vexed, her mother slapped her again.
"Girl, you don't talk to me like that. You are grounded with no food for three nights." She said and locked the teen Louisa in and took the keys away.

Louisa watched herself cry, it was always like that for her, living with her mother was like living in hell. She got starved, beaten, and molested all in one house. If Louisa's mother wasn't hitting her, her stepfather was, and when he wasn't, he was forcing her to have sex with him. This was the night Louisa finally decided to take charge of her life; this was when she made that decision that turned her life around. She watched herself take out a sledgehammer, packed a few of her clothes, broke the window with the sledgehammer in her hands and jumped out of the window. She remembered running for hours that night till she finally got out of town and sought refuge in a church.

Louisa opened her eyes to discover that she was not really asleep, but was down memory lane, remembering her past. She looked around and felt at ease, this was a comfortable environment, a place she was familiar with. She stood up and touched her head, she was running a fever. She laid down and tried to think of what made her get locked up in her memory lane.

She rolled over her sheets, stood up, and went to the window side, opened the windowpane, and sighed. The breeze that blew in was calm and refreshing, it couldn't be better. For that brief moment, Louisa forgot about her past, about being humiliated and subjected to ridicule by Mr. Turner, but it didn't last forever as it struck her that Mr. Turner lacked knowledge of her life, so his critics shouldn't mean anything or affect her in the slightest bit. It wasn't her fault that she made it this far and great by sleeping with men. What was so wrong in sacrificing for success? She thought. It wasn't as if it was a big deal anyways, because, as disgusting as her stepfather was, he had slept with her. So, how bad could it have been with other men?

Louisa remembered the cold look Mr. Turner gave her. She shook her head, just to make the thoughts of it go away, and

Have mercy upon me, O God,
According to Your lovingkindness;
According to the multitude of Your
tender mercies, Blot out my transgressions.
Wash me thoroughly from my iniquity,
And cleanse me from my sin. For I
acknowledge my transgressions,
And my sin is always before me.
- *Psalm 51:1-3*

Chapter 4

> "With the pure you will show yourself pure; and with the devious you will show yourself shrewd."
> -Psalm 18:26

"What is going on with you, Louisa?" Mr. Petkoff, the marketing director, asked Louisa angrily.

They were having a meeting, and at this point, the marketers were giving reports on the sales they had made so far. Louisa had the least sales; even Veronica surpassed her this time. Mr. Petkoff knows her to be good at what she did, but her low sales were getting him upset and confused. She was the top dog, why would she now relax and settle for less?

"Veronica has more sales than you, do you realize that? He yelled, and then turned to Veronica, "No offense, Veronica."

Veronica nodded in silence. They always made her appear to be the worst whenever they made comparison.

"Sir." Louisa started.

"Whatever. Keep your excuse to yourself; I don't want to hear from you. Since when do you have an excuse for laziness? I heard C.T. wholesales aren't buying our product, is that true?" Mr. Petkoff asked.

Louisa didn't know how the information got to him, but she composed herself, looked around the table then cleared her throat. The glaring eyes of her colleagues were all on her, she could bet they were happy she was being scolded.

"It is true sir." She said and bowed her head.

"And you gave up after one trial? Who the hell are you? Marketing is all about being persistent, if you don't know that, know it now." Mr. Petkoff informed, looking at their faces.

Mr. Petkoff stood up angrily. His protruding stomach covered his belt; his mixed colored beard was not charming in any way. He always had a worn-out appearance as if the weight of the world was on his shoulder.

"Mr. Cole Turner, the CEO of C.T Wholesales & Co is a significant client to us, even though he was recently discovered. I don't know what he does and how he does it, he makes money fast. He knows the business. That is someone I am sure I don't want us to lose, more sales means an increase in our salaries." He said as he walked to and fro the meeting room. Suddenly, he turned to Louisa.

"Louisa!" He called.

"Sir?" She said looking confident outwardly yet, she knew she was definitely not ready for what Mr. Petkoff has to say to her.

"You are my best shot to getting Mr. Cole Turner to our side. Go to C.T. wholesales today, market our products and make sure he buys it. Do whatever it takes."

"Yes, sir." Louisa replied.
He turned to Veronica.

"Veronica. Go with Louisa and learn from her."

"What? Sir, that is really not necessary. I mean we all have our techniques and Miss Veronica here…" Louisa took a quick glance at Veronica. She was smiling. Why is she smiling? "Miss Veronica here has her own methods on how she deals with her clients."

It sounded thoughtful, and some of them nodded at what Louisa said. That seemed to be the first time they would ever agree with her.

"That's your opinion, this is my decision. Veronica goes with you. Final! This meeting is dismissed, you all should go out and make sales."

They all left the meeting room one after the other. Louisa looked at Veronica as she rushed to her desk to get ready for their "outing." She could bet Veronica would lecture her on the Bible, then talk about the church activities she attended this week and try inviting her to come for the next one. Louisa sighed and rolled her eyeballs as she picked her bag from her desk.

> "For we are taking pains to do what is right, not only in the eyes of the Lord, but also in the eyes of man." -*2 Corinthians 8:21*

For the fact that Louisa was going back to Mr. Turner was a pain on its own, and that Veronica was her escort was something else. But, she was grateful that Veronica decided not to say anything to her on their way to C.T. Wholesales, although, she cannot guarantee that silence when they would be returning to the office.

Louisa and Veronica sat at the waiting room; the receptionist was less warm and welcoming. That rat! Louisa cursed silently; she guessed he might have told the receptionist of her intentions when she came by. Louisa had been humiliated far too much here, how can Mr. Petkoff do this to her? Make her come back here to receive further humiliation.

Louisa looked at Veronica who had busied herself with reading all the Bible scriptures that were on the wall. The expression of content, understanding, and satisfaction could not be misinterpreted on Veronica's face. She was elated to be here.
"These are glorious verses of the bible, Miss Louisa, look at that one over there, it says…"

"Miss Veronica, I'd rather we keep quiet and be on a professional level here."
"Oh. That's true, but God…."

"Please, I would appreciate it." Louisa snapped and looked away.

What she couldn't understand about Veronica was the radiance that emanated from her whenever she had the opportunity to speak about God. She wondered why Veronica was very good at 'marketing' God but terrible at marketing goods. Those pamphlets she forced into people's hands, the way she talked about God, and many more are at times convincing. Louisa knew if Veronica put her mind to marketing, the way church mattered to her, she would be one of the best marketers the Company had.

"You can come in now. Mr. Turner is ready for you." The receptionist cooed, which Louisa saw as being weird and sarcastic. What did she mean 'he's ready for you now?' Veronica was standing already; she looked at Louisa, who was still sitting down.

"What? I'm organizing myself." Louisa defended herself from Veronica's look.

Louisa sauntered to the office, she wished something could take her away, and she should vanish into thin air or melt, anything to avoid the mocking and judging looks of the handsome Christian brother.

He was warm and welcoming, unlike his receptionist; and what she had expected from him was probably a frown for seeing her again. He smiled broadly to them, shook hands with them heartily and did not have those looks he had on the last time. His eyes weren't judging; instead, they were peaceful. It was almost as if he didn't recognize her. Louisa felt a little bit comfortable, it was not bad.

"Good afternoon sir, this is my colleague, Veronica." Louisa made the introduction, and he shook hands again with Veronica, who was reading the poster on the wall, just above his head.

When they had seated, Louisa gathered all her courage to speak up.

"We are here, again, from Evergreen Skincare and Cosmetics Company, and we have a product to show you. We would really like it if you buy it, here are the samples." Louisa said as she looked at Veronica, who passed the samples to him.

"They are 100% organic, that's what they say, but regardless of this sir, 100% organic or not, it is an excellent product." Veronica chipped in as he collected them from her.
Louisa shot her with killing looks, now she knew why Veronica never made sales. She would not lie.

"Now, that was some kind of honesty I've never seen. I like that." He said to Veronica and looked at Louisa, who looked away. Oh, the shame!
"Miss Louisa, what do you have to say? Why should I buy it? What's my gain?"

Louisa cleared her throat; this was no time to worry about shame or anything. This was business. She looked him in the eye.

"If you have a 50% transaction with us, it guarantees you partnership with the Company. It's like having your shares with Evergreen. This product has a future of great sales as people always do purchase our products, so you can be guaranteed profit on your own part. Apart from that, you get a monthly 2% cut from the sales we make at our Company. We believe that you have in one way or the other done publicity for us and then you get rewarded for it." She stopped.

"Wow, that's impressive. I like it." Veronica smiled.

"Is that all I have to gain?" He said, looking at Louisa. Louisa scoffed, looked away then gave a stern glance.

"Yes. Mr. Turner. I believe that's all the Company has to offer." She replied.

He nodded.

"Okay, what about what you have to offer?" Louisa frowned.

"I am just an employee there. My job is to market their products and relay their messages, that's all."

Veronica looked from Louisa to Mr. Turner, feeling that their discussion was more in-depth than it seemed. Louisa was not finding this funny or comfortable. He just had to find a way to go back to that day. So insensitive!

"Okay. That's great. That's exactly why I'm going to have this product and work alongside with your Company because you realized that as an employee; it is not your job to give out the gains and profit but your Company's." He said as he tapped his table with his pen silently.

Veronica was happy, but lost. What were they talking about? Louisa rolled her eyes.

"Well, thank you. It's an honor." Louisa said to him.
"Yes. It is." He smiled.

Veronica stayed back to talk about the Bible verses, and they both kicked off well. It annoyed Louisa that Veronica can have a welcoming discussion with this fine man while she couldn't have one. Louisa stepped out of the office to give them space to talk Bible while she headed to her car, waiting for Veronica, with the hope that she would be sensible enough to make it quick.

Some minutes later, she saw Veronica being escorted to the car by Mr. Turner. Veronica must be feeling graced right now.
"Thank you for the brief Bible exposition." Veronica said to Mr. Turner as she entered the car.

"You are welcome. I'll be glad to see you on Wednesday at our Bible exposition." He said, protruding his head slightly through the rolled down window of the front seat of the car where Veronica was seated."
"I will be there, Mr. Turner." Veronica said giggling.
Louisa looked at her awkwardly. Is "holy Veronica" flirting?
"Cole is fine." He corrected.
"Oh. Cole, thank you." Veronica said.
Louisa rolled her eyes for the umpteenth time, and this time Cole caught her.

"Miss Louisa, I learned from Miss Veronica that you both attend the same church. I mean, I do come to your church once in a while, and it is a good one." He said.

Something made Louisa feel that he didn't complete his sentence, that he still had more to say. She expected something like: 'it's a good one that preaches the great gospel, but why are you unholy?'

"I think you would enjoy our Wednesday program, you should come." He added.

Louisa saw Veronica nodding. She was definitely not going to be in their Christian romance.

"No, I think I'll pass. Thanks though, for the invite." Louisa responded.

"Oh. Okay, but I'll still expect to see you there, you both." He said and withdrew.

"Bye." Louisa said with no feelings. She just wanted him away.

"Goodbye." He waved.
"Bye-bye." Veronica waved back.

Louisa could not believe Veronica at this point. She shook her head and zoomed off.

"Don't you think you were a little off professionalism?" Louisa asked as she drove.

"Oh? Really? I'm sorry; I just like to meet brethren in Christ." She responded.

Louisa furrowed her brow.

"So, will you come for the Wednesday program? We can go together."

"Just like I said earlier, I'm not coming." Louisa replied icily, not taking her eyes off the road.

Just as if Louisa's refusal created a quiet environment, they both took to thinking.

> But [a] sanctify [b] the Lord God in your hearts, and always be ready to give a defense to everyone who asks you a reason for the hope that is in you, with meekness and fear;
> - 1 Peter 3:15

Veronica still awaited news from the home she registered with as a volunteer; the earlier she got into it, the better, and she really wanted to avoid the blind date her mother had arranged for her. Every of her mother's blind date was nothing to write home about She doesn't know how her mother does it, but every man her mother set her up with is always going straight to the talk of marriage. It may seem to be what Veronica wanted; still, it always seemed too absurd. Wednesday program at Cole's Church was another activity added to her list that she looked forward to and if it really turned out to be spirit-filled, she was never going to miss it in her life. Veronica sighted a couple as they zoomed past them. The man held on tightly to his wife like she was going to be taken away by someone else, and they looked so happy. It reminded Veronica of her lonely life, no companion. She knew God was in control, and she was going to leave it up to Him.

Louisa watched Veronica sigh repeatedly, and it really pissed her off. Louisa thought, if this would keep Veronica quiet, let her brood all she wants. Louisa stole a quick glance at Veronica, and she thought her to be prettier when she was younger. She remembered the event from earlier; recalled how Veronica's smiles didn't dry off as Cole spoke to her. Even the holy ones flirt. Cole was charming, that could not be disputed, which made Louisa wondered how much of a playboy he was; but he was a Christian, and from his actions, he looked like a sincere and devoted one. Louisa smiled at the thought of kissing those pink lips on his face. She knew most of the girls in his Church would have eyes for him. Wondering how he looked and acted in church or among his Christian brethren made Louisa conclude to go for the program on Wednesday so she could see things for herself. She was definitely not going with Veronica.

> "But we have renounced the hidden
> things of shame, not walking in
> craftiness nor handling the word
> of God deceitfully, but by manifestation
> of the truth commending ourselves to
> every man's conscience in the sight of God."
> -2 Corinthians 4:2

"Hey, we are here." Louisa announced as she parked her car, jerking Veronica out of her thoughts.

"Oh, thank you for the ride." Veronica appreciated her as she made to step out of the car.

Louisa nodded; this was the only opportunity she had to ask for Cole's church address, she didn't want a situation whereby Veronica and her would be having the "give me Mr. Turner's church address" conversation in the office.

"Veronica." Louisa called her name with a stop.
"Yes?"
Louisa was not sure how she would start, the fact that she had stood her ground earlier that she wasn't going made her feel uncomfortable asking for the church venue. Besides, Veronica was definitely going to request they go together.

"Mr. Turner seemed very nice, I don't know what transpired between you two before but why wouldn't he agree to buy the products earlier?" Veronica said with one of her foot outside and the other still in the car.

Louisa frowned. If she had the slightest idea that Veronica was going to bring this up, she would not have held her back.

"We still have a report to give. Right now, we are almost at the end of the day's work, so I suggest we hurry to the office to report the outcome of our sales today." Louisa said, concealing the anger in her tone.

Veronica nodded; she understood Louisa didn't want to discuss her previous meeting with Cole.

"Yes, that reminds me. You called my name earlier; did you have anything to say to me?" Veronica asked her as they walked side by side to the primary office building.

Yes. I wanted you to give me Mr. Cole's church address, but you just had to bring up a very heartbreaking memory to me with your dumb question, Louisa thought to herself.

"Louisa!"
Louisa turned, in response to the call of her name, concealing the fact that she was almost lost in thoughts.

"Yes. I did call your name, I just wanted to say you should uh." she was clearly out of words. "Try to be less sincere when marketing." She added as quickly as possible.

Any discussion that would lead back to Cole was definitely not welcomed for now. So, asking for the address was not needed presently.

"I appreciate your tips, but lying is something I don't do, even our Father in Heaven doesn't like it. As children and lovers of God, dishonesty should be far from us. Lying is against the ten commandments in the Bible. It is a sin. Our God is honest in all His ways, and we, as His children should emulate Him."

Louisa rolled her eyes and stopped as they got to the front of the office. Veronica had to understand something in the business world.

"Look, Veronica, I get it. I get it that you are this great, perfect and 'commandments abiding Christian', but this is business. When it comes to marketing, your religion and some basic morals should step aside. Really."

"Dear…." Veronica started.
It got Louisa's brows worked up.

"In everything we do, God is involved, that is why we do not forsake Him in any way. I will correct you on something, I am not a great, perfect and 'commandment abiding Christian' as you have described me. I am a child of God, one who loves Christ first before being a 'commandment abiding Christian.' She said making air quotes and then chuckled.

"You also can be a dutiful Christian, the one that abides by the commandments too because you love God. Dishonesty, lies, they are very dangerous. Have you heard of the story of Ananias and his wife, Sapphira in the Bible? The book of Acts chapter 5 talked about them. These people were wealthy enough to own land, now they decided on their own to sell this land and use the gain from it in the house of God. After the sales, they hid half of the money and took the other half and laid it at the Apostles feet, thinking that no one would know but the Apostles knew, and he asked Ananias why he had allowed Satan to fill his heart to lie to the Holy Ghost. Do you know that Ananias fell down and died immediately? His wife too died not long after. That was how this couple became the architect of their own death. There are many more examples like that in the Bible, and these things happen in our everyday lives. We are lucky because God loves us, and He is slow to anger. His son, Jesus Christ has come to…."

"Stop!" Louisa barked. They stared at themselves for a while. "See you inside." Louisa said and walked away from her.

She knew that if she listened to any more of what Veronica had to say, she might have some self- tormenting questions for herself later, and that is the last thing needed on her radar at the moment. Veronica was so good the way she started her preaching thing, because it so much caught Louisa off guard that she almost settled down to listen. Louisa scoffed as she thought of why Veronica couldn't make high sales with her persuading talent.

And we know that all things work together for good to those who love God, to those who are the called according to His purpose.
Romans 8:28

Chapter 5

> **"Oh, do not remember former iniquities against us! Let your tender mercies come speedily to meet us, for we have been brought very low."** -*Psalm 79:8*

Veronica has been waiting anxiously for the Happy Home for the old and retired people she registered with to assign her to a particular duty. She was there the previous day, and they had an orientation for everyone who volunteered to work with the Home. She was surprised at the turn-up of volunteers and how happy and ready they looked for the occasion. The speaker gave them all the information they ought to know and be familiar with. Veronica felt honored with the much and exaggerated appreciation they were given for being volunteers. After the orientation, volunteers were distributed to different sections and people staying in the Home, but she and two others couldn't get a placement. In the meantime, they joined others to do their general work in the kitchen while expecting to be assigned later. Just working for the first day gave her so much joy and relief that she couldn't wait to have a private placement.

Veronica was arranging some files on the shelf they all shared in their office when her phone suddenly rang; she hurriedly picked the call when she saw it was a call from the administrators of Happy Home.

"Hello, Veronica Sanders speaking." She answered pleasantly with a smile.
It made Louisa and a few members of the office look her way, she sounded like she was on a millennium call.

"Yes. I can make it by five. Thank you very much." She replied to whatever had been said at the other end and hung up.
Louisa cannot help but notice the radiance that came with her smiles. It left Louisa wondering what kind of call made her feel that excited. Veronica was something else, and Louisa knew that because even though Veronica looked like someone with the weight of the world on her shoulders, she was still happy. There was always something that gave her great joy and happiness.

"Hello." Veronica greeted Louisa as she passed her to return to her desk.

Louisa had barely opened her mouth to respond when Veronica got back to her desk looking very cheerful. Louisa was not ready to listen to any preaching from Veronica, but she was eager to be at the program Cole had invited herself and Veronica to. It was the next day, and Louisa still hadn't figured out the venue. She dreaded asking Veronica because she didn't want to have to snap at her when she started her sermon.

"Ma'am." Lillian called her.
Louisa adjusted herself on her chair and looked straight at Lillian, who wore a stern and harsh look.

"Mr. Petkoff asked that you see him now."
She nodded.

"I will be there shortly." Louisa said and waved her hands for Lillian to leave her side. Lillian was good at handling people, and she knew how to get information from others. She would be an excellent tool to use to get Cole's venue for the program.

"Hey, Lillian." Louisa called her to a halt.
"Yes ma?"
"Can you do me a favor?" Louisa whispered to her as she came closer.
Lillian nodded.

"Good. I need to know where Mr. Turner would have a program tomorrow evening. Can you help me find out from Veronica? She got invited."

"Okay ma, I will." Lillian assured her.
Louisa nodded in satisfaction, waited for Lillian to leave then stood up and went to see Mr. Petkoff. She really hoped he wasn't going to ask that Veronica went with her for her marketing and sales today.

After the day's work, Veronica hurriedly left the office and boarded a cab to the Home. She had prayed the previous night that God should make her get a placement that would favor her, for her to make a difference. Smiling broadly at everybody and anybody, Veronica walked into the Home. The old and retired people there seemed all glowing and healthy this evening. It wasn't like the first time she came around when it was as if they all had too much to bear, but this evening they were pretty much engaged. Those that were not playing games were either having conversations with nurses and volunteers or having a group talk with their fellow Home mates. The atmosphere was infectious with happiness, and Veronica could feel it.

The administrator at the Home welcomed her with a smile as she stepped into her office.

"Welcome, Miss Veronica. How are you today?"
"I'm good. God is great." She replied.

"Nice. Anyway, I will cut to the chase. We've got placement for you just as I said earlier when I called you. Here." She said and handed Veronica a file and continued. "I'm sure since you volunteered; you are already prepared for whatever challenges that may come with the work. Now, if you don't want to do the work, no qualms and no one is going to push you to it."

Veronica looked from her to the file; she opened it to see what information it carried. From the name to the information on the owner's background, it got Veronica's world worked up. At first, she thought she saw wrongly, but after looking at it for over five minutes, she knew it was clear.

"Mr. Kwame Dion is a good and happy man. He lost his legs in a car accident where he lost his sister. Things have been really hard for him. Gratefully, Mr. Kwame is getting better and better. I personally think he needs someone to help him. Though, he has nurses, I still feel there is a need to have someone who would be of help regardless. I believe you would really help him out. I mean judging from what you wrote in your form and from the character and manners you have exhibited."

By the time the administrator stopped talking; Veronica had beads of tears rolling down her cheek.
"Oh! Dear. Don't cry. Life is just like that, I mean not everyone gets to be satisfied with what life has to offer, so we forge ahead notwithstanding."

Veronica didn't know if she cried because she knew Kwame Dion, or because of pity for him, or because she had no idea such evil can befall him. Then again, she didn't want to believe it was the same Kwame Dion she knew.

"So, we need you in your free time to go work for him in his house. He wouldn't be staying here. Can you do that?' Veronica sniffed repeatedly, wiped her face and then, nodded.
"Yes, I can."
"'That's great. Mr. Kwame is around if you want to meet him."
Veronica knew that more than anything right now, she wants to see him, but she wasn't sure how he would react to her. He probably won't recognize me, she thought and shrugged.

"I will love that."
The administrator smiled and patted her back.

"That's nice of you. Come with me." She said and Veronica followed her as she led the way.

Veronica walked icily, there was a heavy weight on her legs and it made it tough for her to carry her own legs. She looked around and saw the people there locked in their present preoccupation, they looked like they had nothing to worry about.

The administrator entered a room which was separated from the rest and it looked more decorated. There was a wheelchair in the room; on the wall were landscapes posters and flower pots placed at the window side. On the bed was an old man laughing to whatever has been said by the person occupying the wheelchair. The occupant on the wheelchair in the room backed them as they entered the room, Veronica remembered Kwame as funny also, and if he hadn't lost his style then she was not really surprised if the old man laughed out his fake teeth.

"I see you two are having fun." The administrator smiled and walked up to them, then stopped as the wheelchair turned to her.
"Mrs. Katherine, how are you doing? I've been to your office earlier but you were not in." He said with so much ease.

Veronica thought he was better than she expected, she was expecting to see an emotionally broken down Kwame but this was not the case, he was still handsome as she could recall. She slowly traced her eyes down to his legs and what was written in the file was right. She had silently wished it wasn't true. Her throat went on a real painful lockdown for trying to hold back the tears that almost streamed down her face. It was sad that his long athletic legs were gone.

"Yes, I was busy with some people. How are you today sir?" The administrator turned to the old man that just nodded, rubbing his hands sweetly.

Veronica saw how the administrator was with them; she was sweet, real, genuine and compassionate. It left Veronica wondering if she could do it.

"Anyway, I came with someone. The person I discussed with you." She said and they both turned to Veronica. She took it as her cue to walk up to them.

He looked at her and she knew he still recognized her. She held her breathe and feared that if she talked she would burst out in tears. She smiled.

"This is Mr. Kwame. Mr. Kwame this is Miss…"
"Veronica Sanders." He said in delight.
The administrator looked at them both.
"Hello Kwame." Veronica said with a plain smile.
"Wow, it's been years. What is it? Thirteen, or fourteen years?" He asked surprised. He probably tried to hide his astonished tone but he wasn't doing a good job anymore.

Veronica laughed, stooped to hug him and gave him a peck.
"I see you two know each other. Uh, why don't we leave Sir to rest here without disturbing him?" The administrator said pointing to the old man who had fallen asleep already.
"Sure." Kwame said and they left the room.

Veronica and Kwame fell into an awkward silence as the administrator left them to talk at the garden.

"I can't believe I'm looking at you right now. My goodness!" He finally said.

She nodded. "How have you been?" Veronica asked him.

He smiled, sucked in a great deal of air and shook his head. He looked at her, he could tell where her question was coming from, she was wearing a concealed worried look but he knew the kind and meek Veronica too well. He looked away from her.

"I'm good. I've been doing great; actually, it has never been better." He said as he let out a painful smile.

Veronica couldn't hold it any longer; she let her tears roll down.

"Kwame, how did this happen? Last time I heard about you, you were working in Las Vegas." She said amidst her tears.

He watched her cry and waited for her to stop. Only if tears could give him back his legs but that would not happen. A lot of people had cried and felt sorry for him but it was not going to do anything.

"Please, Veronica. Stop crying. This was in the past. I don't live in the pains of the past, you shouldn't." He said taking her hands.

She sniffed hard, took out her handkerchief and mopped her face. She looked away from him. She was mad at herself for crying in front of him, she was sure she had made him feel bad and that was definitely not what a volunteer do. A volunteer shouldn't spread sadness, which she knew.

"Veronica, things happen and what is meant to be will be. I blame no one for my predicament, not even my carelessness. Everything has been predestined by God and He knows what He is doing. Jeremiah 1: 5 say, "Before I formed you in the womb I knew you; before you were born I sanctified you; I ordained you a prophet to the nations." God has our lives planned for us and all we have to do is listen to Him." Kwame said with so much vigor and no regrets.

Veronica was still trying to process the whole situation. It was shocking that Kwame was not only saying the scriptures but also talking about God. A lot must have really happened to him over the years. The Kwame Dion that she knew never really liked listening to anything about God. What happened?

"I was stupid, young and dumb. Do you know the only thing I regret? I regret not taking God seriously when I was younger." He smiled and looked at her again. She was blank and he knew she was clearly lost. So, he continued. "I lost my legs five years ago and believe me when I tell you this, it was not easy. I was a man with legs that works perfectly fine and then the next minute, it was gone like that, in the twinkle of an eye."

Veronica felt as if her heart was going to explode; it was very heavy as if a great load was dumped on it, not comparable to the way she felt when she was following the administrator to meet him.

"While I was working at Vegas, I was really notorious with money and ladies. You think I was bad when I was a teenager, you should have seen me in Vegas. I lived like there was no God; no one seems greater than me. Money? I had enough and I got so drunk with it. When 1st Timothy 6: 10 said; for the love of money is the root of all evil, it wasn't a joke at all. It further went on to say, which while some coveted after, they have erred from the faith, and pierced themselves through with many sorrows. Veronica, I really pierced myself with so much sorrow. My sister, Kimani shouldn't be the dead one. I should." He said in tears, and so much pain.

Veronica watched him cry, poor Kimani! She thought. She patted his back and hoped it would soothe him in anyway.

"I slept around with women and took so much pleasure in it, and I also did drugs and was into it full time. Kimani dissuaded me from it but I was adamant to the core, telling her I was living my life while I still can. But, I was so wrong. One of the ladies I slept with was the girlfriend to a feared gangster in the hood then, but I didn't mind. I knew and I thought I was lord over them because I had the cash. I had a little gang of my own too. What kind of drugs didn't we take? Heroine was breakfast, lunch and dinner. I was an addict to drugs and weed. With time, the gangster came challenging me for sleeping with his woman and threatened to kill me. I didn't mind, I felt I was untouchable. Our gang had a clash for that and we fought. In the fight, I lost two of my dearest friends and I was barely over that two weeks later when I was informed that Kimani was taken hostage by them. I went for my sister, to rescue her but I couldn't. On getting there, I was beaten to a pulp and tied down. My sister was raped before my very own eyes, repeatedly."

"O my God! Kimani!" Veronica exclaimed now in tears.

"I managed to free myself and fight our way out of

there, as I drove, I couldn't bear to look at Kimani. I was so heartbroken, bitter, and sad. I just felt my whole world crumbling. I lost control while driving and ran into a ditch that made my car summersault and then it went ablaze. Boom! That was the end. I don't know who took me and how I got to the hospital, I woke up to hear the bad news, that my sister was dead and me, no legs." Kwame burst into tears.

> **"Do not remember the former things, Nor consider the things of old. Behold, I will do a new thing, Now it shall spring forth; Shall you not know it? I will even make a road in the wilderness And rivers in the desert.** - *Isaiah 43:18-19*

Veronica tried calming him down but it was difficult, she was in tears too. Kimani was a very beautiful, nice and sweet girl. Growing up, she and Maureen had been her favorites. Maureen would be so heartbroken to hear the news.

"Kimani paid for what she knew nothing about. My iniquities were visited upon her. Exodus 20:5b." He said and shook his head.

"Visiting the iniquity of the fathers upon the children unto the third and fourth generation of them that hate me." Veronica quoted the part of the Bible he said silently.

"If I had loved God then just as I love him now, none

of these would have happened. I would have still had Kimani but look at me now." He bowed his head.

"God loves you more than you know. Stop blaming yourself because Jesus has washed our sins on the cross of Calvary. He has forgiven you of all your sins and that is greater. You are a new creation now in Christ. Truly, your past cannot be deleted but you have to forgive yourself so that you can live with yourself." Veronica pacified him.

He nodded and looked up into the sky. There were both quiet for some minutes and Veronica felt as if she was suffocating.

"I'm glad I met you today, I haven't felt this light since Kimani's death. I've never discussed it with anybody. Even when I was in rehabilitation and when I was going through therapy but I'm glad I could share it with you easily." He said smiling.

Veronica smiled lightly.
"Come on! We shouldn't be feeling down and low today, we haven't seen for years now, we should celebrate instead. I'm sorry for dampening your spirit." Kwame said in a happy mood.
"No, it is fine. I'm actually glad you shared this with me." She replied him.

"How is the family? Maureen and Ann?" He asked.
"Maureen is married with kids now and Ann is still in college." Veronica answered feeling guilty for talking about Maureen's marriage; Kimani would also have been married if she were alive.

He nodded. "That's just great. Uh, how about Juliet? Is it? No, uh Jill?"

"You mean Janet?" Veronica laughed.

They never really got along well, Janet didn't even like to see his face in their house back then.

"I'm sorry. I couldn't recall her name, how is she?"
"I don't blame you for that. She's good."
"So, volunteer? Why?" he asked her.
"Should there be a reason for it? I don't think so."

They chatted for a while, catching up on each other's life. After a while, she insisted that she take him home and they left the Home after saying their goodbyes to the administrator.

> See then that you walk circumspectly, not as fools but as wise, redeeming the time, because the days are evil. Therefore do not be unwise, but understand what the will of the Lord is.

Chapter 6

> As one whom his mother comforts,
> So I will comfort you; And you shall be
> comforted in Jerusalem." *Isaiah 66:13*

Veronica rushed into her old Volvo car to her mother's house. Her mother had called her earlier that she should come over for dinner. It was not Monday, so she wondered why her mother made it seem so necessary with the way she sounded. Ever since she met Kwame, she had really not been herself, still shaken at how life works differently for everybody.

"You are late, as usual'." Janet said immediately she opened the door.

"Why do you get to be the one that answers the door every time?" Veronica asked as she entered the house.

"That's because she neither helps with cooking nor the setting of the table." Maureen answered Veronica's question as she hugged her.

They laughed, but Janet didn't. Instead, she scoffed and went away. Veronica sighed. Things have still not gotten smooth between them, it had actually gone from bad to worse since the dinner they had their outburst. Veronica knew she had tried on her own part to reach out to her, but Janet was doing her possible best to shut her out.

"Where are your kids?" Veronica asked Maureen as she dropped her bag on the armchair. The house seemed unusually quiet.

"They are at Tom mother's house. I'm taking a break from them for a while, you know?" She said, pointing to her stomach. "It's great, I mean Tom and I have enough time to ourselves now." She added.

"Well, I think you guys have enough time to yourselves with or without the kids, considering the upcoming baby." Ann, the youngest of Veronica's sisters, said coming out of the kitchen carrying a bowl.

"You are back." Veronica exclaimed.
Ann ran to her after she dropped the bowl on the table. Janet rolled her eyes, irritated as they hugged themselves, Ann didn't hug her like that when she came in. Maureen didn't

seem all that excited to see her and their mother had been making one complain or the other about her.

"Welcome, Love."
Veronica followed Ann as she entered the kitchen; their mother was busy stirring the soup in the pot. Veronica hugged their mother from behind.

"How are you doing, ma?"
"Fine. Now that you're here, take over the soup. I need to do something else." Her mother said and handed her the spatula.

After the preparation of the food, they settled down to eat at the dining table. It was only their mother, Veronica, Janet, Maureen and Ann just like old times. It reminded Veronica of when they were younger; she missed how much it used to be them, alone against the world.

"Why did you call us for dinner, mother? Is there something you have to say to us?" Janet questioned, raising her fork.

"Should there be something before I have dinner with my girls? I missed having dinner like this, it's been long." Their mother replied.

They all nodded except Janet, who just chuckled. They had the rest of their dinner sharing events from the day's work.

"Ann, are you through with the semester's examination? The last time we talked, you told me that examination would be starting soon." Veronica dropped her plates in the sink and then turned to Ann, who was behind her.

"No. I just came home briefly; I felt like being in a homely environment, and besides, mummy kept on insisting that I come." Ann replied.

They all turned to their mother who didn't dignify their present attention with a look; she continued her food without looking away from it. Janet could swear that she caught her dancing slowly and almost invisible as she ate.

"Mother, you look suspicious." Janet alleged bluntly. While the children nodded in agreement with Janet, their mother dropped her spoon slowly then looked at them, turning her gaze to them one after the other.

"Now, what's suspicious about having dinner with my girls? This is how it supposed to be."
Veronica noticed it was upsetting her.

"Yes, exactly, Mum. This is how it is supposed to be, and we all appreciate you for your thoughtfulness. It is just like old times and its bringing back memories, we love it." Veronica winked at her sisters.

They continued in silence, they all probably had different memories that kept coming back. Veronica was locked up in one of hers as she remembered when she was seventeen, and they had a youth program in church. The program ended late that Kwame had to drive her and Maureen back home that night. By the time they got home, her family had started dinner, and Kwame was persuaded to join them. It was her mother's way of showing appreciation to him for his kind gestures. She recalled how after dinner, she invited him to her room, and after talking for a while they became engulfed in their little teenage romance, which didn't last for long time because Janet had rudely interrupted. Veronica laughed out loud, remembering how embarrassing it was.

"Vero. Vero! Why are you laughing?" Maureen asked as she nudged Veronica.
She was a bit shocked as she looked around and just realized they were in the kitchen.

"What?"
"You look so happy, are you seeing someone?" Maureen asked her quietly so that Ann would not hear them.

"I do? Well, the joy of the Lord is my strength."
Maureen nodded to it and continued peeling the orange in her hands, Veronica had a pineapple in hers, but she wasn't cutting it. It was almost as if she was out in space, Maureen smiled, and knew something was really going on.

"You know you can tell me anything." Maureen told her. "Pass the pineapple to me."
Veronica gave it to her.

"Yes, do you remember Kwame?" she asked Maureen, who still concentrated on what she was doing.

"Who is Kwame?" Maureen asked, paying no attention.
"High school Kwame." Veronica hurriedly said as if dropping a bomb.
Maureen paused.
"Oh, Kwame. You mean your forever crush and only love Kwame?"
"What do you mean my only love?"
Maureen gave her a mocking look and sneered at her.

"Anyway, what about him?"
"We met."
"You met?" Maureen dropped the knife.
"Yes, I mean, I met him. We talked."
"Go girl! Is he married?" Maureen quickly pushed it in before her sister snapped and stopped talking about him.

"I don't think so. Wait! What has his being married got to do with me. Maureen, don't get any silly ideas in your head. We are all adults now."
Maureen laughed.

"Yes, and who said I was getting any ideas, I just asked a question everyone back from our high school would ask. I mean everyone wants to know if the player can ever settle."
"Oh, really? Look Maureen, things are different now. I mean, his legs are gone."

"What do you mean?"
"He is crippled." Veronica said with a pain in her heart.
"What?!" Maureen yelled.
Veronica nodded as they both fell silent.

> **And make straight paths for your feet, so that what is lame may not be dislocated, but rather be healed.**
> *Hebrews 12:13*

> "Judge not, and you shall not be judged. Condemn not, and you shall not be condemned. Forgive, and you will be forgiven." -*Luke 6:37*

Louisa was all dressed up for the program; she purposely delayed all that she did. She wanted to avoid being there at the start of the event so that she could enter graciously. She took the paper Lillian wrote the address in. She smiled as she thought of how smart Lillian was, Lillian pretended to want to follow Veronica to the program, and Veronica suggested they go together for this one then that was it! She gave her the address.

Louisa smiled as she entered the Chapel; it was small and filled up already. She had to occupy a seat at the back, and she wasn't comfortable with that. She looked around if she could see Cole, but instead, she saw Veronica smiling and waving to her from where she sat. She smiled back to her and decided not to look her way again.

As the preacher was welcomed to the pulpit, Louisa saw Cole in his black trousers and grey shirt, his sleeves were rolled up, and she could tell he came directly from his office. She watched him usher the preacher to the pulpit, and he was looking so dashing. Louisa quickly looked around to see how the ladies were staring at him, especially Veronica.

"Today, we are going to talk about forgiveness. Can someone say amen to that?" The preacher said immediately he got upfront.

"Amen!" the congregation chorused.

"Yes, Amen. Forgiveness is easily accessed, but we fail to use that powerful key to get to our Father in Heaven. How many times have you forgiven this week? How many times have you told someone that I forgive you for what you have done to me? Luke 4 verse 4 says, forgive us our sins as we forgive those that trespass against. We say this all the time but do we mean it? This is our Lord's Prayer that we recite, but we do not abide by it. I need us to understand the good that comes with forgiveness. I tell you today, you cannot hold on to the past offenses of people and then expect to really do well yourself. Forgiveness gives us peace, it aids tranquility. There is a satisfaction you get when you hold no grudges against nobody. You want God to forgive you for your sins, and you have not forgiven your neighbor for messing up your lawn. You have not forgiven your friend that offended you. I pray to God to have mercy on us." He paused and wiped the sweats from his forehead.

"Amen!" the congregation chorused again and became silent immediately.

"When I look back to the years, we humans have sinned so much that if God were man, we would have perished a long time ago, but he is God!"

"Yes! Amen!" the people shouted.
He continued.

"Let's open our Bible to Acts 26, verse 18. Are we there? I will read it now. To open their eyes, and to turn them from darkness to light, and from the power of Satan unto

God, that they may receive forgiveness of sins, and inheritance among them which are sanctified by faith that is in me. God's intention for us is not to perish, but he wants us all to reign with him in the kingdom at the end of it all. We should turn our hearts to God and ask for forgiveness. Forgive the people around you, show mercy. Matthew 6:15 says if ye forgive not men their trespasses, neither will your Father forgive your trespasses. Brethren, the Bible has said it all. Forgive those who offend you, those who have cost you so much pain, and probably great loss. Just let it go and forgive them."

As he talked on, Louisa got more and more sunk into his words, her heart was heavy as she remembered her mother and her beastly husband. The pain they've cost her made her come this far; regardless of that, they have put a stain and tainted her life, and she could not just let it go. Her poor father was hurt too, he tried his best, and it wasn't his fault he wasn't rich. All her mother could have done was stay by his side to help him, but apparently that was too much for her to handle. Now, this man of God says she should let go of the past, forgive and move on. Never! She wasn't going to do that; she would forever hate her mother.

"Let's bow our heads to pray." The preacher finally said, and the whole congregation did as he asked, everyone except Louisa.

After the service, Veronica made sure to catch up with Louisa as she left the church premises.

"Hey, I didn't think you would come but I'm glad you did." Veronica said pleasantly.

"Thank you." Louisa replied.

Veronica looked around. "I actually invited Lillian; I would have loved it if she came. It was so blessed. Were you blessed...?"

"Good evening, ladies. I am so happy you both made it. For a while there I thought Miss Louisa wouldn't make it. I hope you enjoyed the service?" Cole asked when he finally got to them. He saw Veronica during the sermon and thought he should greet her after the service. He was more excited when he sighted Veronica talking to Louisa outside the Church.

"The service was great, I was really blessed. Thank you, sir, for the opportunity you gave me to be here." Veronica appreciated him.

"Sir? Please, Cole is my name, call me that. God gave you the opportunity. Miss Louisa." He called and smiled at Louisa.

All this while he had talked with Veronica had been talking, Louisa did nothing but admire him. She was so lost in her fantasy that she wasn't paying attention to him.

"Yes, the service was quite something. Forgiveness is good, right?" She turned to Veronica, who nodded in return. Veronica looked at her wristwatch and gasped. She had to be with Kwame now, and she was running late.

"I would love to stay and chat, but I have to be somewhere, thank you, sir. I hope for more invitation to programs like this. Miss Louisa, see you tomorrow and please take care." She said, and the next moment, she was out of sight.

Louisa returned her gaze to Cole, who was still fixed on the direction Veronica took.

"I forgive you, Cole."

He turned to her and gave a somewhat confused look as he put his hands in his pants pocket.

"You forgive me?" He asked.

Louisa started walking to her car. He followed her.

"Yes, for the insults you gave me the first day we met and for revisiting the issue indirectly, trying to spite me when Veronica was present." She said with a frown. It still annoyed her whenever she thought about it.

He laughed a little.

"I'm glad you have forgiven me. Thank you."

She made a face at him and entered her car. He peered in through her opened window.

"What are you doing on Saturday? Are you free?" He asked her.

Louisa had an inner blush. He wanted to ask her on a date.

"My schedule is booked for the weekend." She said, trying to play hard to get.

"Okay. Well, here's my card. Eventually, if you are free, just call me." He handed the card to her.

She took it from him and made a quick glance at it. She looked at him.

"What's this? Are you trying to ask me out on a date or something?"

"Date? No, there is this function for children at the orphanage. I just felt you might like to be there, it is usually great. The kids there are wonderful." He assured her.

"Too bad, I'm not a lover of motherless babies." She replied.

"Really? I guess you must resent me then."
She felt guilty, but what did she care anyway.

"Sorry about that, but I will try to be there, if I can, and see how these babies are going to make me love them." She said, trying to clear up her guilt.

"It is fine. Whatever pleases you. Do have a nice quiet time tonight." He replied.

"Quiet time?" That got her lost.

"Yes, your devotional time with God." He shed more light on it.

"Oh! Anyway, goodbye. Have a nice quiet time also." She said and ignited her car.

He watched her drive away. When she was out of sight, he went to his car and drove away.

> **Delight yourself also in the Lord, And He shall give you the desires of your heart** - *Psalm 37:4*

Louisa got home, tired, and exhausted. The thoughts on her mind on her way home, mixed with the preacher's words, made everything seem hard. She really wanted to throw away his words so that they would have no meaning to her, but she couldn't and the longer she had it in mind, the more she meaningful it got and the more she saw the need to forgive her mother by letting go. Louisa had all the money she wanted. She was a successful marketer, and her life was good; what more?

Her phone rang out, and it brought her back to reality. She took it out of her handbag, saw that it was an unknown number, but she didn't mind. Right now, all she needed was someone to talk to.

"Hello Louisa Allen speaking." She said, but the caller went dead silent, she looked at the phone, and the call was still on, but no one was talking.

"Hello, is anyone on the line? No one? Okay, bye." She said, and hung up.

She threw the phone on the chair. This kind of prank call was not something she needed at the moment. She needed someone to talk to, she had no friends, no family, and she was so alone. She couldn't possibly talk to her dog, it couldn't speak. As she stood up to go for a shower, her phone rang again; it was still the same unknown number. She growled as she picked up the phone to answer the call.

"Look here, I've got no time for strangers' pranks. I advise you stop before I report you to the Police." She roared.

"Louisa, this is Chris, your stepbrother. I advise you come and take your Momma before she dies here." The caller revealed.

Louisa stuttered. "What? Chris? What the hell? I have no Mama. Deal with your family problems alone and stop involving strangers." She barked and hung up.

The call was one of the worst calls she had ever received in her life, if not the worst. How did he get my number? She asked herself. Everywhere became so hot for her, and she started sweating profusely, even with the AC on. She picked her keys and decided to go for a walk and do anything to erase the event that just happened. She did not even want to spare one minute to think about it. What does he mean? 'Come and take your Momma.'

"Bullshit!" she cursed.
Louisa walked down her block; people around looked too busy and happy. They looked like they had no problems of their own, but she knew it was just a facade, everyone had their problems, and they would eventually have to deal with it. She stopped at a coffee shop and decided to chill there for a while; she went on Facebook and searched for her mother. From her post, she looked thrilled; so what does 'Chris, your stepbrother' mean?

Louisa looked outside from the pane glass; she didn't care about any Chris or her mother. She saw Veronica across the street laughing, she was with someone on a wheelchair, and they were talking happily. Without thinking or giving it any thought, she paid for the coffee and ran outside to meet her.

"Veronica!" Louisa called to her.
Veronica stopped and turned to her. It was then Louisa thought of what she was doing. This was the same Veronica she didn't like to be seen with or associated with, but it was too late as she had already turned to her and Veronica was already giving her the wide and charming smile.

"Louisa, quite a surprise. What are you doing here?" she asked.

"Yes, I live around here. Just came out to have coffee and then I saw you."

"Oh. Good, are you okay? You kind of look disturbed." Veronica asked, as she noticed her sagged eyes.

Louisa looked at the person on the wheelchair, handsome guy, too bad he was stuck to the chair. Veronica followed her eyes.

"Sorry. Kwame, this is Louisa, my colleague at work and Louisa, this is Kwame." Veronica said plainly.

Louisa smiled and saw why Veronica had left the Chapel in a hurry.

"Nice to meet you, Louisa." Kwame said and stretched his hands for a handshake, she shook his hands.

"The pleasure is all mine." Louisa replied with a smile. He seemed nice.

"We'll be leaving now. Goodnight." Veronica said, and started to leave.

"Wait!" Louisa hurled.

They stopped.

"Do you care for late coffee?" Louisa asked not sure if she sounded desperate.

Veronica was surprised. First, Louisa was talking to her, and now she was asking her to coffee. She looked at Kwame, who nodded.

"Okay. That would be nice."

"Great, come with me." Louisa said, and they made for the coffee shop.

"So, you mean to tell me she was also a bore in high school? Gosh! I can imagine her nerd and geek look." Louisa laughed out loud.

They were visiting memories of Veronica and Kwame's high school days with Louisa, and she was clearly enjoying it.

"I was not a total bore. I was in the school choir. I sang." Veronica defended herself.

Louisa shook her head. "Why don't you join the church choir? I mean you would look good in those purple robes, you know." She took up her mug and sipped from it.

"You attend the same church?"

"Yes." Veronica answered.

"Great. It reminds me of your Momma back in the days. She sang in the choir too, didn't she?" Kwame asked. Veronica just nodded.

"You know, I found it weird when Janet wanted to join the teenage choristers then. She was just so not it." He continued.

"Janet?" Louisa asked not wanting to be left out of any gist.

"My sister." Veronica laughed, remembering that time too. Janet had insisted she wanted to join, but her mother had refused because she knew the motive behind it was to spend time with one of the choir boys.

"Janet had a motive. My mother knew about it; that was why she didn't let her."

They all laughed like they understood what the motive was. Louisa was having a good time, and she barely remembered she had a very unwanted call earlier, but the buzzing of her phone reminded her. She looked at it and saw a message from 'Chris, her stepbrother.' She frowned, and her countenance fell. Veronica noticed it, but she didn't want to ask or be a bug.

"Are you okay?" She still asked.
Louisa looked up from her phone and nodded.

"Just dumb messages from dumb people." She replied, but nobody found it funny, not even herself.

They chatted more, and they slowly drifted into the sermon they received from the program they attended. Kwame helped shed more light on forgiveness, although Louisa enjoyed it, it pricked her more and more. It was an excellent time with both of them, especially funny Kwame, but she couldn't bear to continue the discussion.

"Let's see how many people there are to forgive this week. I have to go now; it was really nice talking to you two. Thank you, Veronica."

"Thank you for inviting us to coffee. I mean, we paid for it but thank you." Kwame said, and they laughed.

They bid themselves goodbye, and Louisa left them behind. Louisa cried as she walked home. Her father was dead, but she wished he was alive, there were things she would have loved to do for him. Yes, he contributed nothing to her life, but unlike her mother, he still cared and showed some love.

It was really tough starting her life on her own, and she resented her mother for it. Now her mother thought she could just walk back into her life like that? She didn't care what happened to her mother in her husband's house, all Louisa knew is that she should live there and die there too. Her mother was definitely not getting help from her. Since she got herself in there, she should find her way out of there herself.

> But whoever listens to me will dwell safely, And will be secure, without fear of evil."
> -*Proverbs 1:33*

> Fear not, for I am with you; Be not dismayed, for I am your God. I will strengthen you, Yes, I will help you, I will uphold you with My righteous right hand.' - *Isaiah 41:10*

Chapter 7

> "He heals the brokenhearted
> and bandages their wounds."
> -Psalm 147:2

Kwame was outside at his garden enjoying the cool breeze; it was refreshing as it took his mind off some disturbing thoughts. He smiled as his mind drifted to Veronica. She was still as kind and pleasant as she was back in high school. Her knowledge of Christ made her more appealing to him. Veronica had always been a devoted and true Christian. He looked at his wristwatch; she ought to be there with him anytime soon. He was grateful she had chosen to volunteer and that fate had brought her to him again. This time around, he wasn't sure he could let her go.

Veronica announced her arrival by calling out his name when she couldn't find him anywhere inside the house. It took a while before she figured he was in the garden, walking to him made it seem to her as if she belonged to him. It was a weird feeling to her, but she felt it. She felt owned.

"Hey. How are you doing?" She asked him as she got to where he was.
He smiled at her, nodded and closed his eyes.

"I'm really fine." He opened his eyes and turned to her. "Thank you for coming into my life again."

She was also grateful she was in his life too; she felt her cheeks turn red and as if it was going to come off, she cupped her cheeks with her hands.

"Have you had dinner?"
"No. Not yet."
"I will fix you something now." Veronica said and turned to leave.

He caught her by the left hand and pulled her back with little energy. She turned to him.

"Just stay. We can do that later, maybe order out or something. Remember, men shall not live by bread alone but by every word that proceeds out of the mouth of God." He quoted from the Bible.

Veronica smiled. She sat down on a bench not too far from her. He pushed his wheelchair closer to her, so that they now faced each other.

"Would you like to attend a Bible study with me sometime next week? It is always amazing."

"That is just the right thing I need. I will, you can count on that." He assured her.

They fell silent for a while, with Veronica miles away thinking. Strangely, Louisa came to her mind, especially when she thought of the night they had coffee together, she could tell she was going through some difficult moments and she needed someone. Veronica sighed at the thought of it, everyone had their own problems and sometimes they make it look as if they were doing perfectly fine whereas they were dying inside. Who would have thought Louisa, who always snapped at her, would be the one to invite her for coffee. She remembered that the next day, when she saw Louisa at the office, she looked so distant, distracted and unenthusiastic about the new products that were on ground.

"To be honest, there are times I just want to give up. This life is really tiring; I mean I do wonder how Job in the Bible did it in his time. He was so strong willed and concentrated on God, in spite of the temptations from friends and his wife. That he lost everything was enough reason to backslide." Kwame suddenly said, bringing Veronica out of her subconscious thoughts.

"Job was really blameless, even God knew and that was why he allowed the Devil to mess around with him. Faith was something Job never lacked; he had mastered his faith in God. He knew where he was heading with the Father, he trusted God too much to give up." Veronica added, after giving it some thoughts.

"Job's faith is something that is missing in this contemporary world. We give up, even before it starts. Sometimes, we forget that as Christians, we would face tribulation, but God never gives us something that is too much for us to handle. Look at Abraham and the only son he had in his old age, Isaac. Abraham was willing to sacrifice Isaac as God had ordered. He knew the God he served; he trusted and had faith in Him."

"Yes, Abraham was really a father of faith. Every man that exercised faith in the Bible was never abandoned by God; He rewarded every one of them in one way or the other. Hannah and Sarah are good examples too. I am sure that at a point they must have gotten fed up, but Hannah didn't give up. Hebrew 11:11 says, through faith also, Sarah herself received strength to conceive seed, and was delivered of a child when she was past the age of childbearing, because she judged him faithful who had promised. That Sarah was able to judge God faithful means she trusted God. We need to put our trust in God; I need you to trust God too much to give up. He has a whole lot in stock for you." Veronica said.

Kwame nodded. Veronica knew he started this conversation probably because he was feeling frustrated about the whole situation going on his life.

"Thank you, Veronica. I will do my best to trust Him too much to give up. It's getting cold outside, let's go in."

> **"Finally, brethren, whatever is true, whatever is honorable, whatever is right, whatever is pure, whatever is lovely, whatever is of good repute, if there is any excellence and if anything is worthy of praise, dwell on these things."** -*Philippians 4:8*

Louisa on her part was yet to decide if she would be going to the children program Cole had invited her to. Yes, she wanted to see him but she couldn't let herself to be so small before him. It was one thing that he turned her down like no other man had done, and it made her run wild with curiosity. What kind of man was he to turn her down like she was nothing close to appealing? She decided to go and have a shower and make her final decision to go or not, while at it.

Since he had given her his card, she had never let go of it for more than five minutes. Even at the office, she clung to it like her life depended on it. After her shower, while she dressed, her phone rang; it was still the same unknown number. Why he won't stop calling was what Louisa couldn't comprehend. She believed she had made it clear enough to him that she didn't have anything to do with her mother, and perhaps she had not made it clear enough to him. She picked the call and started furiously.

"I thought I told you not to call me? That I ignore your text messages means I don't want to talk to you; neither do I want to talk to her. So stepbrother, take care of your father's wife. I mean, she has lived all her life with you. Why bother someone who barely knows her?"

"That's not why I called. Can we meet?" He said calmly. He didn't sound harsh like the first time they had talked on the phone.

Louisa paused but she deeply craved to know why he called.
"So why did you call?" She said from her end.
"It is better said in person. Let's meet up."
"That is not happening. If you can't say it now then goodbye, I don't care about your family crisis." She snarled.

"I'll forward the address to you and I would like it if we could meet up. I'll be expecting you regardless of your refusal to come." He said and hung up.

That took Louisa by surprise. She should be the one hanging up and not him. Why was he so hell-bent on pulling her into their family matters? She was not interested and she wasn't seeing or meeting with him anywhere. His call had set her on edge, so she sat on her bed, angry.

Why would they intrude into her life at this point? There were times she had needed family by her side, but they were not there. She chuckled at the thought that they might be in need of money and needed her help. If that was the case, this was the day she had worked so hard for, the day she was going to flaunt her money before her mother and still do nothing to help her. She recalled when she was fifteen and how she came across her father and discovered he was sick. Even against his wish, she had gone to her mother and pleaded that she helped him with money, but she had doggedly refused, without giving it a second thought. Her mother was so heartless, she can never forgive her for that, but this time, she was going to meet with 'her stepbrother' to hear what he has to say, but just once.

In the next few minutes, Louisa's phone buzzed. It was a text message bearing the address of where he wanted to meet her, a well-known coffee shop. Louisa was satisfied with the location. It was an open place; no harm could come to her. She reluctantly dressed up and headed out to meet him.

By the time she got there, she looked around and till she saw a man waving to her, and beside him was a woman; her mother. Louisa frowned, but she was happy that she had dressed elegantly enough for the meeting. She raised her shoulders even more as she walked to them.

Chris pulled out a chair for Louisa, who she smiled briefly at him as she sat down. Her mother looked away, not able to bear looking at Louisa, and Louisa, on her part, did her very best to ignore her mother by acting as if she was not there.

"Mr. Chris, I'll advice you hurry up with whatever you have to say." She was blunt with her words.

Chris looked at her mother and she knew that her mother was the one that put him up to it. She waited impatiently for what she had to say.

"Louisa." Her mother called her name, sniffed and tried to reach for her hands that were places on the table.

Louisa withdrew her hands, placed them on her laps and finally turned to her mother.

"Miss Louisa, call me with titles. We are not familiar enough for you to call me by name; and madam, please hurry up with whatever you have to say and don't put up any act of self-pity and righteousness." Louisa harshly let out what she had burning on her lips.

Her mother sniffed even more, Chris held her tightly and she sort of rested on him. It was not visible, but Louisa could see it clearly that they had each other to lean on. Something she never had, something she yearned for greatly. A mother to be her backbone, a mother to listen to her, a mother to hold her when the whole world would not; a mother to have her back when everyone had turned their back on her. Louisa couldn't bear to look at them anymore; she looked away and battled with holding the hot tears that burned her eyes greatly.

Chris took the cue to leave them alone to talk; he stood up and went to a different table.

"I know what I have done to you, the pain I have caused and the hatred I've put in your heart, are unforgiveable and no matter what I say, I can never be justified, but Louisa, I beg of you, this guilt that I have carried on for the past years has eaten me up to the point where I feel I'm going to drop dead at any moment. Please." Her mother said, tears rolling down her eyes.

Louisa chuckled. "I really don't have anything to say to you. Yes, the punishment for your sins is death. You are responsible for the death of my father, and you know that because I came to you for help and you turned your back against him, against us. You should really die; I will visit your grave." Hate and pain was all that filled the tone of her voice.

Louisa stood up and looked at her mother. "I came thinking something bad had happened to you, I really wanted to rejoice over that but seeing you here, alive and healthy angers me. Enjoy your miserable life."

On that note, Louisa left. Inside her car, she couldn't drive straight away because she was consumed with so much anger and hurt, every part of her heart hurts her really bad. She found it hard to breathe as she tried to hold the tears that had reached the top most level of her eyes and the wails that wanted to come out from her mouth.

When Louisa finally felt calm, she looked into the coffee shop through the open glass, and saw Chris consoling her mother. She frowned and wondered how a beast like her could have someone by her side. Not wanting to see the affection between mother and son, she drove away speedily.

Back home, she flung everything that came her way and broke several glasses. She picked and dropped every flower vase she owned, breaking them to pieces. She kicked all the things that obstructed her way. In her room, she tore apart her curtains, scattered her books, and threw her PC on the floor. She pulled out her duvet and threw them away. She screamed real hard, pulled her hair and cried. Louisa screamed till she almost lost her voice; she wanted to shout her lungs out.

Her heart was sad, and she was mad at herself even more, because at the sight of her mother, she couldn't deny that she felt the urge to embrace her, cry on her shoulders and tell her how hard it had been for her. Louisa wanted to know if her mother had been doing so well but that was not how it was supposed to be. She had stayed all these years trying to forget what it felt like to have a mother, and when she just started feeling very comfortable with the situation, her mother suddenly showed up.

Louisa's phone rang out, but she was not ready to speak with or see anybody, so she took out the phone and switched it off. Solitude should comfort her. It had always comforted her.

> **Bearing with one another, and forgiving one another, if anyone has a complaint against another; even as Christ forgave you, so you also must do.** - *Colossians 3:13*

> **"I will give you back your health and heal your wounds, says the Lord."**
> *Jeremiah 30:17*

Veronica ran into the hospital like she was being chased by a lion. At this stage, nothing counted or had meaning to her. Janet had called her while she was at the office that their mother was found unconscious in her living room and she had been rushed to the hospital. On getting there, she met her sisters, Janet and Maureen. She couldn't really get answers from Janet's expression because her expressions were stiff. She looked at Maureen, who ran to her immediately she noticed her presence. Maureen was in deep tears, so Veronica could tell that things had gone really wrong.

"What happened? Maureen? Where is Mum?' Veronica asked restlessly.

Maureen just kept on sobbing.
"Janet? What is going on? Is she okay?"
"She's got cancer. She is in for surgery and radiation therapy. She would start Chemotherapy when the Doctors say so." Janet said coolly.

"Chemo what? My God! Cancer? How?"
"She's got it for a while now." Janet informed.
"And you knew?" Veronica asked angrily.
"Yes, but recently."

"You didn't think to tell me, to tell us." Veronica yelled.
Janet sighed and stood akimbo.
"She didn't want you to know."
"Well, I do now. Happy?"

"Calm down, Veronica. I'm sure it was for the best. Janet means well and this is not the time for anyone of us to lose it. We have to be there for one another and for mother too." Maureen intervened.

Veronica knew that, but she was just too upset, this was so sudden. She couldn't even tell her mother was going through something like this. She went to Janet and embraced her.

"I am sorry. Thank you for doing as she wished." Veronica said still holding unto her.
Janet felt at ease, she also needed this embrace. She could not be acting strong every time, being comforted at times like this was something she needed. She reciprocated the embrace.
"I'm sorry for not saying anything." Janet also apologized.

Maureen was not going to be left out, so she placed her hands around both of them as she sobbed on.

> **And the Lord will take away from you all sickness, and will afflict you with none of the terrible diseases of Egypt which you have known, but will lay them on all those who hate you.**
> - *Deuteronomy 7:15*

After some hours, they were allowed to see their mother. Veronica cried as she saw her mother lie down on the bed looking very pale. It was so scary and she couldn't hold back her tears. She waited for her mother to talk, to say anything, but she was too weak to do that. Veronica held her hands and closed her eyes, and when she opened them, her sisters were by her side, all looking at their mother who tried to smile but they were far too weak to convince anybody that everything was going to be fine. Veronica mobbed her face and sniffed, she took Janet's hand into hers, as she was the one standing next to her.

"Let us pray." She said plainly.
Janet looked at her, Veronica nodded to reinforce what she had said, and she didn't just say it but she meant it. Janet took Maureen's hand and Maureen held her mother's right hand. They closed their eyes.

"God, we thank you because you are there for us. Your only son, Jesus Christ has taken our sins away on the cross of

Calvary and you have washed us clean in your blood. You are the God that heals the sick, you are the God of possibilities and you are a God of wonder. I pray that you, o God would lay hands your on my mother. You would heal her of every disease. You have said it in your word that by your stripes, we are healed. Jesus, we ask for your healing power. Bestow upon mother today, strength and healing." She paused.

"Amen." Her sisters chorused.
"Amen." She added and let go of Janet's hand.

They opened their eyes and looked at their mother; she had fallen asleep during the prayers. They all sighed and their hearts were heavy, but Veronica had made up her mind to trust God too much to give up. She had faith that everything was going to be all right.

> "That if you confess with your mouth, "Jesus is Lord." and believe in your heart that God raised him from the dead, you will be saved. For it is with your heart that you believe and are justified, and it is with your mouth that you confess and are saved." -*Romans 10:9-10*

Louisa was feeling bad for not returning any of Cole's calls, and for also standing him up. At least to her, she thought of it as a date, even though a lot of little children would be there playing around. She didn't mind the children being around, as long as she had him to herself, to study and seduce. She laughed out loud.

Taking out her phone, she picked his card and dialed his number.

"Hi. This is Louisa." She said immediately the call was answered.

"Yes, wow. It is very nice to hear from you. How are you?" Cole said in his perfect gentleman nature.

"I'm fine. I'm so sorry about Saturday. I was so occupied, I couldn't come, and I feel like I stood you up." Her fingers were crossed.

"Stood me up? No, no. you didn't. I had a lot of fun with the children. I'm even sorry you missed it, it was wonderful." He said from his end.

Louisa rolled her eyes; he just had to rub it in her face.

"Well, then. Where are you?" Louisa said and bit her lower lips.

He was silent.

"Wait, it came out wrong." She tried justifying herself. He laughed. "No, it didn't. Anyway, I'm running late, I have a church program to attend." He informed her.

"Oh." She let it out like a hiss.

"Will you like to join the program? You would love it since you loved that last program you and Miss Veronica came for." He said.

She agreed without giving it a thought, just an excuse to see him.

"Great, I will text you the address now. Oh, can you help me reach out to Miss Veronica. It slipped my mind; I should have informed her earlier about it."

Louisa frowned, why would Veronica be in the picture?

"No problem. Text me the address as soon as possible, I don't want to be late too." She said and smiled as if he could see her smiles, then she hung up.

The text came in; she stood up from her chair in the living room to get ready for the program. She was definitely not going to reach out to Veronica. Louisa thought Veronica should miss this one. It was not like she could attend all the programs in the world; not all belongs to her.

Immediately Louisa got to the church, she saw Cole. He was ushering people in and welcoming them. He ushered her to a seat at the back not too far from him as she came a little bit late and the front pews were occupied already. After the praise and worship session that really got everybody on a high spirit, including Louisa, the congregation sat down and the sermon started after a song ministration.

"Repentance is what we are going to be talking about today." The preacher said holding onto the microphone tightly. "Somebody say repentance." He ordered.

"Repentance!" The congregation, including Louisa, echoed, and it made her wonder if there was a kind of illusion she was seeing. She looked at Cole, but he wouldn't spare her a look. His face was so stern that it was obvious he was already lost in the message even before it started.

The preacher continued.

"Repentance is to turn from evil and do good. In Christendom, repentance is turning to God and giving up on your sinful ways. I don't know if you know this, but there is no repentance without the confession of your sins. When one is guilty of various sins or a sin, he must confess in what

way he has sinned, in order to receive atonement and forgiveness. God created the earth and filled it with beautiful things that would satisfy mankind, which He created in His own image, but Adam fell short and was thrown out of the garden of Eden. Even at this, God still loved us with all his heart. Despite our sinful and immoral acts, He didn't mind, He still opened his arms, waiting for us to run to Him; but what have we paid Him back with? Sin. More and more sins. In the love that he had for us, and for our redemption, He sent His only begotten son, Jesus Christ to come and die for our sins. For sins the son did not commit, he came in flesh and blood to us, suffered pain, shame and death, all for the sake of our salvation." He paused and mopped his face. The congregation was still and silent.
He went on.

"The same we, who Jesus had left his throne for to come and save, scorned him and put him to death, but He did not relent because of the love of the Father for us and the Love which he also bore for us too. He paid the debt He did not owe. We owe the debt, but we couldn't pay, we needed someone to wash our sins away and that He did. Jesus is calling on us today for true repentance. Now, true repentance leads a person to say, 'I have sinned.' True repentance requires the humility of the heart, the broken spirit of sinners, the true mind and desire of God. True repentance is not asking the Lord for forgiveness with the intention to go back to sin again, it is not asking the Lord for mercy, with the intent to go back to lie, to fornicate, to hate, to hold grudges, to be jealous or to look for the downfall of people, no! True repentance is a honest, regretful acknowledgement of sin with the readiness and dedication to change. Repentance leads us to cultivate godliness while we do away with habits that leads to sin. Amen?"

"Amen!" They chorused again and went silent.

"Matthew 4:17 says, 'From that time on Jesus began to preach, 'repent, for the kingdom of heaven has come near'. The kingdom of God is near; do not let people tell you, it is still a long time from now. I tell you, build your life in Christ starting from today. When he comes, I am not going to be judged for your sins, you are not going to be judged for mine. In Matthew 21:32, the Bible says, 'John came to you to show you the way of righteousness, and you did not believe him, but the tax collectors and the prostitutes did. And even after you saw this, you did not repent and believe him'. Sometimes, we are so adamant that we refuse to accept Him. It is not that we are oblivious or ignorant of God but we just choose not to accept and believe in him. John 3:16 has said, 'For God so loved the world that he gave His only begotten son and whosoever that believeth in him shall not perish but have everlasting life'. Believe me or not, it is better to have everlasting life in God than to perish in hell. We have been given the kingdom; let us claim what is ours. We are heirs of the Father, we have been given access to all the riches and glories, and all we need to do is believe and accept Jesus Christ today."

Louisa was in tears, she was no more in her physical consciousness. Her heart wept, her soul wept and her body wept. She had been a sinner filled with numerous iniquities. She had not found her way with Christ, yet, every first Sunday she would go to church and make big donations to show off. God did not even accept it and she thought she was right all along.
The whole congregation was sober now.

"The book of Acts says, 'Repent, then, and turn to God, so that your sins may be wiped out, that times of refreshing may come from the Lord'. What is that thing that you are going through? What is that thing pulling you down? Come to the Lord for refreshing, come and lay your burden at the feet of the Lord, come and open your heart to him. He is your Father, he listens to us, and He would never neglect the righteous. Open up your heart to him today, ask that He cleanses you. Don't be deceived by the Devil, don't be his tool, do not be manipulated by him. 'The thief cometh not, but for to steal, and to kill, and to destroy: I am come that they might have life, and that they might have it more abundantly', Jesus said this in John 10:10 while teaching with parables. Who is the thief? The Devil, but Jesus has come to give us life abundantly. And why? Open your Bible to John 14:6. It says, Jesus saith unto him, 'I am the way, the truth, and the life: no man cometh unto the Father, but by me'. Brethren, today, Jesus is calling unto us, He is begging that we come to the Father who has given so much to us, who has showed us boundless love, a steadfast love with no limits. He doesn't want us to perish and that is why it is said in the Bible that Heaven rejoices over one sinner who repents. Let us repent today and change our ways. Let us pray." He said.

The congregation stood up with hearts that want to be turned to God for good.

"Say this prayer with me. Dear Lord, thank you for your forgiveness, despite all that I have done. Thank you for constantly reaching out to me. Thank you Jesus for dying for my sins. Thank you for showing an endless love to me as you keep on calling unto me to repent of my sinful ways. Help convict me of my sins and help me accept your mercy without shame. Today, I am confessing my desperate need for you, help me and make me live in you without blemish."
"Amen!" They all chorused.

The preacher came down from the pulpit, and just as if it was planned, the new converts went on their knees to pray. They cried and wailed.

Louisa wept tirelessly. She found it hard to believe that even after all she had done, she could still be forgiven of her sins. After sleeping with numerous men for sales, lying and making sales through dubious means? Would God still cleanse her for hating her mother so much, not letting go of her sins and for wishing her mother evil? If God could have mercy on her, if He could overlook her sins and still welcome her into the kingdom, who was she not to let go of the past and forgive her mother?

She cried even more as the choristers sang a song of redemption. Louisa made the conviction in her heart that she was never going back to sin again, she was going to live a blameless and upright life that would glorify God in Heaven.

> **The Lord is gracious and full of compassion,
> Slow to anger and great in mercy.
> The Lord is good to all, And His tender
> mercies are over all His works.** *Ps. 145:8-9*

> **But God, who is rich in mercy, because of
> His great love with which He loved us,
> even when we were dead in trespasses,
> made us alive together with Christ (by
> grace you have been saved)-** *Eph. 2:4-5*

Chapter 8

> "Therefore if any man be in Christ, He is a new creature: old things are passed away; behold all things have become new." -*2 Corinthians 5:17*

Louisa walked into her office feeling brand new, there was this kind of clean and fresh air she felt around her ever since she encountered Christ. She greeted Veronica and everybody in the office with a smile; it gave her so much ease, comfort, and acceptance. If she had known that this feeling of satisfaction could be attained in Christ, she would have gone to Him a long time ago. Her always heavy heart was lighter than it ever was.

Lillian walked to Louisa's desk with some files resting on her right arm; she looked smart and simple, yet bold and braced up for the soon to be unleashed anger by Louisa. Louisa had indeed gone out of her way to be friendly, unlike her usual self for a few weeks now. But, Lillian was not going to be deceived by whatever charade Louisa has going on.

"We will have a meeting very soon, say, in the next thirty minutes." Lillian said, carefully and patiently picking her words.

"I believe I could have been told earlier. Anyway, it is okay."

"I am sorry ma'am." Lillian apologized.

"It is okay." Louisa replied her.

After the meeting, Veronica came to apologize to Louisa for not being able to follow her for the day's sale.

"Veronica, I've told you it is fine. Your mama needs you, go to her." Louisa said, smiling. She meant to hold Veronica's hand and give it a little comfort squeeze, but she thought it would seem like going overboard.

"Thank you. I will see you tomorrow." Veronica said and made to leave, but stopped as if she left something behind. "You know there is a Bible study program tomorrow in the church, right?" She reminded Louisa who she thought would have probably forgotten.

"Yes. Thank you."

Veronica nodded and went to her desk. She packed her bags and exited the office; she drove to Kwame's house to pick him up. He had insisted the previous day that he wanted to see her mother. Next stop was the hospital for them. As they got to the hospital, Ann was the first person to see them. Even in her tired state of hours of crying and watching their mother, she still ran to her sister when she saw her.

"Welcome." She said quietly.

"How are you? Have you eaten?" Veronica asked, and she shook her head. "You know you have to eat, anyway, where is everybody?"

"Maureen went for a checkup, so it's just Janet and me." Ann replied, and then looked at Kwame, who Veronica was pushing on the wheelchair.

"Forgive my manners, Kwame. How are you doing?" He smiled and waved his hands.

"No, don't worry about that. I should be the one asking how you are doing. You are looking thinner. Let us go and get something for you to eat." He said, grabbing her wrist.

"You shouldn't bother sir. I will be fine, you can just check on Mummy while I sort myself out."

"That is not a bad idea, but you need to be monitored while eating. I want to be sure you would eat."
Ann laughed.

"Thank you, Kwame. Ann, I think you should go with him." Veronica said and let go of his chair.

Ann nodded. She looked at Kwame, who was giving her a very encouraging smile, and then she followed him as he led the way of pushing his chair himself. Veronica sighed as she watched them go. The week had really been exhausting, but thanks to Kwame for being a source of strength to her. She felt as if he was the one on volunteer services, not her. They had gotten really close over time; they made decisions and move based on each other's opinion. Even though the time was tough, Veronica still had time to smile, Kwame made sure of that.

After Veronica had examined her sleeping mother in the best way she could, she retired to the couch in the room. Kwame had transferred their mother to a VIP room. At first, she refused, but with his constant persuasion, she just had to let him have his way. Janet, who went to ease herself earlier, came in to join her on the couch.

"Do you think she is getting better?" Janet asked Veronica, who had her head in the air. "Veronica! Are you lost or something?"
Veronica jerked, awake from her preoccupied mind.
"Sorry, I didn't catch that. What did you say?"

Janet looked away from her. "I bet you couldn't. Never mind. Anyway, I would be out of town for the weekend, I'm taking Jake on a road trip."

Veronica thought she did not hear her right, so she had to repeat what she had said to be sure.

"A road trip?"
"Yes, and before you judge me. I have my reasons. It is not like I just want to see my mama lay on the sick bed and then go out and have fun with my teenage son who doesn't know his father."

Taking note of her word, Veronica took some brief seconds to examine her. She looked really worn out, and as if she had a lot on her mind. The lackadaisical look she always had on was buried beneath her eyes.

"I'm sorry for almost judging you, I just felt we all have to be here together for 'mama' in case something goes wrong. I guess I'm selfish and inconsiderate that we all have our different lives and you have your family to keep up with. I'm wrong." Veronica said calmly.

"You are damn right." Janet said, looking at their mother; she placed her hands on Veronica's. "But nothing is going to go wrong. Mama would be okay." She said to reassure her, and it comforted Veronica, making her wish that Janet was always like this.
"Janet, are you okay?"
"Yes, I am." She said, letting go of her sister's hand.

"Please, you can talk to me about anything. I want you to, please." Veronica pleaded, looking straight into her sister's eyes.

Janet smirked. "That's you and Maureen thing, running to each other and telling each other. I was always left out, so, I'm kind of used to dealing with things myself. Thanks, though, for the offer but I'd rather not be judged and criticized by you." There was pain in her voice.

Veronica knew Janet was right because she never really gave Janet the attention she gave Maureen. Janet always had this withdrawn wild attitude, and it was hard for Veronica to keep up with it; she was sorry for being the kind of person Janet thought she was. She was sorry for being judgmental.

"Janet, I'm so sorry. None of those claims is my true intention, I love you very much, and all I always want for you is the best, nothing more. I just don't really like it when you go wild with your decisions, and then you make awful mistakes, whereas you can get the best in the world."

"You think Jake is an awful mistake? Are you saying Jake is not the best for me?" Janet was getting angry.

Veronica quickly held her hands and made Janet turn to her.
"That is not what I'm saying. Jake is actually one of the best things that happened to us all. He is family."

"I don't think so." Janet pulled her hands from Veronica's. "You always do this, you always find a way to refer to the circumstances that led to his birth and then you clothe it in a way that seems as if you are the righteous one here."

"Janet."

"No, that's the truth. Fine, I made a mistake. I was young but why do you always rub it in my face." Janet stood up.

"Janet, I have never done that. Never ever and I would never do that. You and I both know you still haven't forgiven yourself, and that is why you, my darling, make way to go back to that history lane whenever you have the chance, and you put the blame on somebody, anybody. Unfortunately, I have always been the one shot with the blame bullet." Veronica explained gently to avoid offending her further.

Janet looked at her, her eyes were so red, and they were ready to let down a stream of tears. She quickly turned away when the first drop trickled down her face. She couldn't let Veronica see her like this, she walked to the window side and had her back turned to Veronica.

Veronica let her stay alone for some minutes, probably to cry or wallow in her own thoughts. She stood up from the chair and hugged Janet from behind.

"Family sticks together always, and I don't mind taking all the blame bullets, I want you to just know that I am here for you always and forever." Veronica said, still hugging her.

Janet sobbed a little loudly now, she felt at rest and was ready to let it all go. Guilt has always stayed with her and Veronica was right, she still hasn't forgiven herself, and she took it out on Veronica. She was an easy target anyway, Janet was extremely sorry for putting Veronica in that position, and she couldn't imagine how sad she felt every time she made her the villain in the story.

"I'm sorry, Vee, I am truly sorry." She said and turned around as she properly hugged Veronica.
Suddenly, their mother coughed. It was not loud, but the room was quiet enough for them to hear her. They ran to her bedside.

"Mum." Veronica said, smiling even though tears were still flowing.

"Janet." Their mother said lowly.
"Mother, I am here." Janet said, taking her hands.
Slowly, she closed her eyes and went unconscious.
"Doctor! Doctor!" Veronica screamed and ran out.

She came back shortly with a doctor and two nurses that seemed very eager. They excused both Veronica and Janet out of the room. A few minutes later, they were rushing their mother to the emergency room; they followed the doctor and nurses but were stopped at a particular point. For forty minutes, they were still in there with all the doors locked; nobody was coming out to say anything.

Ann cried all through, she was at this point regretting why she had not spent enough time with her mother. Kwame could do little to comfort her, Janet paced about aimlessly like a ghost.
Maureen came rushing to where they were.

"Veronica, what's going on?" She asked, holding her sister's dress.

"I don't know. One second, mother was awake, the other she was unconscious, and they just rushed her here to the emergency room without saying anything to us." Veronica said. She wanted to cry, but she had to be strong for her siblings. Kwame held her hand tightly and squeezed it lightly.

"Sit down, Maureen." Janet ordered. "You can't be getting stressed out in your condition; we can't afford to lose you too."
They all stopped sobbing and turned their attention to Janet.
"What do you mean lose me too? Who are we losing?" Maureen asked, charging at Janet.

"I'm sorry for not telling you this before now, but Mum just has two months to live." Janet said in a shaky voice.

Maureen couldn't believe what she just heard. She staggered, and Ann ran to support her, and made her sit down while Veronica stood up.

"How long have you known this?"

"That's how I found out she has cancer. The dinner we had together that last time, she organized it on purpose. She wanted it to be kept away from you all, especially Maureen." Janet explained.

Just then, the doctors came out.

"How is she now?" Kwame asked, when he noticed that none of the sisters wanted to ask for fear of the worst.

"She is still in a critical condition, but she is stable for now. You know as the day draws by, it gets more and more challenging. She will be transferred to her room soon, so don't worry about it too much." The doctor said, and walked away.

Veronica battled with her eye lids as she tried fighting the tears to hold it down but couldn't. She sat down mindlessly on the chair and cried her eyes out because it was still unbelievable that her mother had only two months to live. Had she known, she would have listened to her mother earlier about her getting married and wouldn't have been so adamant and stubborn.

> **"Let all bitterness and wrath and anger and clamor and slander be put away from you, along with all malice. Be kind to one another, tenderhearted, forgiving one another, as God in Christ forgave you."**
> *-Ephesians 4:31-32*

Louisa had called Chris, her stepbrother to bring her mother out so they could meet. She was not sure if she was confident enough to forget all that her mother had made her go through, but Cole had encouraged her all the way. She was sure she was going to forgive; she had even forgiven her since the day she gave her life to Christ.

She waited patiently in the coffee shop, where they had met previously. Events from that day filled her memory and played over and over again.

"Hey." Chris said as they got to her.
"Hello, Chris. How are you doing?" She asked him, smiling.

She looked at her mother, who was looking very sad and feeling left out, so Louisa stood up, drew her mother close, and embraced her. That took her mother by surprise to the extent that it wasn't until she had processed the whole situation before she held her daughter tightly. They both felt the warmth of satisfaction and acceptance. It was really natural for Louisa.

"Sit." Louisa said as she pointed to the chair opposite her. Her mother obliged. Chris went away to another table to give them alone time to pour out their minds.

They were silent, her mother was probably thinking of the best way to put express her apologies in a way that won't get her angry like the last time. Louisa took her time to observe her mother; who was so lean and looked sick. There were visible marks of bruises on her left cheek and her neck.

Louisa was displeased by the sight of this because even all these time of hating her mother, she had always hoped she would be okay and doing fine.

"Louisa, I really appreciate it that you took out time from your busy schedule to see me." Her mother started.
"I'm not that busy." She replied honestly.
Her mother sighed.

"What I have done to you, the pain I have caused is unforgivable, and I know how much you resent me, but please, forgive me. I am not asking you to forget, and I am not going to make excuses for myself. Even if you don't have me back in your life, just give me the assurance that I can live the rest of my life thinking about you without having guilt chunk out the life in me." She stopped; her face was wet with tears, and so was Louisa's.

"Who am I not to forgive you? We are humans, and we all make mistakes. To err is human but to forgive, mother, is divine. I am just a mere man, I have my faults too. If God can let go of my sins, and forgive me, I see no reason why I shouldn't do the same. So, you have the right to think of me, and you are going to be a part of my life, just as I will be a part of yours, henceforth."

Her mother burst into uncontrollable tears, she tried her best to console her. She was happy, and she felt good about herself.
"Thank you. You will never regret this decision, and I promise to make up for the years I failed you."

"Thank you for reaching out to me too."
Louisa beckoned to Chris to come and join them at the table.

They drank their coffee together, and while Louisa gets to know Chris better, their mother just stayed quiet and watched them happily. She never thought a day like this would come, when she could be so close to Louisa and watch her laugh heartily without minding who was there, or without remembering the grievous sin she had committed against her.

"How about your husband, my stepfather." She said with a firm push, referring to him as her stepfather still did not feel right to her.

Her mother and Chris both went silent.
"Mother has been through hell with him, especially after you ran away." Chris said.

Louisa looked at her mother, who made a very pitiful look.
"Mother?" Louisa called her, and it could be seen that she wanted to know everything.

"This is a happy moment, let's not ruin it." Her mother said lowly.

"I insist." Louisa pressed on.
Her mother looked at her, if not anything, she still remembered Louisa was self-willed, stubborn, and adamant.

"That night, when we discovered you were gone, it was then it dawned on me how useless and stupid I was. I accused him of being the cause of your fleeing, but he turned it on me. Somehow, we got into a heated argument some days later, and that was when he shamelessly told me he abused you sexually and he doesn't feel sorry for it. I tried to fight him, but he beat me up that I fell sick for days; I thought I was going to die. He threatened me with you, he said he had found you, and if I misbehaved, he was going to kill you and me. I was scared, I knew I had lost every right to you, but I was also sorry for being such a useless and bad mother, the least I could do was protect your life from him. So, I did all he wanted and all he ordered. I was his sober medication; whenever he was drunk, he would beat me to a pulp and life was just unbearable, but I knew I was paying for my sins, and that I deserved it all. I had to find you, and when I did, I saw the difficulties you were going through with money and all. That was why I had to do what I had to do. I was the one in charge of the scholarship you had while in college, but I couldn't let you know. I was too ashamed." She paused.

"Oh, mother."
She continued. "Presently, he is dead. I killed him."
"What?!" Louisa shouted alarmed.
Her mother sobbed. "I am sorry. I will be going to prison soon, but I don't want you to hate me, or see me as a criminal. Even though I am a criminal, especially if we consider my crimes to you."

"Mother." Louisa called sadly. "I forgive you for everything, it was in the past. I forgive him too. Sometimes, we are controlled by vices we do not know of."
"Thank you, but no criminal under the law will go unpunished."

Louisa shook her head and held her hands.
"We will fight this. I promise you.

> **"But seek first his kingdom and his righteousness, and all these things will be given to you as well."**
> -Matthew 6:33

Louisa was assigned to go and market the company's new product to a fellow skincare company, which had shares in Evergreen Skincare and Co. They were significant stakeholders in the company, and that was why Louisa, the best marketer, was put on the job.

Louisa was not sure of her ability to carry out this work, but she had to pull it through. She was a marketer before she started sleeping with buyers and using dubious ways to get them to buy the products; but most importantly now, she was a Christian, a child of God and a vessel for use by God. She trusted God, and she knew that whatever the outcome, positive or negative, it is the will of God.

She walked confidently with grace into the office of the CEO of the company, he had asked that she directly come to market to him.

"Good morning sir." She greeted as she got into his office.

He smiled crookedly. "Please, sit. What would you like to have?" He asked as she sat down, placing the sample wares on the table.

"Nothing, I'm fine. Thank you." She answered him.
"Oh, well, then. What do we have here?" he said, pointing to the samples on the table.

"These are the new hair products. I know we always deal with skincare products, but the company has decided to take a new step, and I can assure you, just like always, you will not be disappointed." She said and looked at him, as she picked one of the samples and passed it to him.

"I am sure I won't be disappointed truly." He said with a grin and winked at her.

"This product, I can guarantee you is hundred percent natural and organic."

He stood up from his seat and came over to her.
"Stop!" He said and placed his fingers on her lips.
She pushed his fingers.
"I beg your pardon, sir."
He frowned and then smiled. He briefly ran his hands through Louisa's neck.

"Babe, come on. Stop acting like you don't know what to do. Come on, we'll make it brief here then we can continue at the hotel we usually meet."

Louisa slapped his hands away from her laps.
"I won't do that. I won't sleep with a man to market my goods."

He chuckled. "You are so funny, then what will you call what we did the last time? Dancing with me?" He asked huskily.

Louisa shivered in embarrassment. She looked straight, not wanting to grace him with a gaze.

"That was before, this is now. This is a new me, a new creation in Christ. I have submitted this body, my body, which is the temple of God to Him, and only God is entitled to this body because He is the love of my life." She objected firmly.

"So what are you saying because you sound gibberish? If I want this entire attitude, I would have asked for someone else. That plump lady, what's her name?"

Louisa shot him a killing look but still tried to play it cool.

"I will now continue to tell you about this product, at the end of it if you do not want to buy, fine. I will walk away and if you want it, good for us all." She said with without delay, no smiles, no friendly outlook.
He frowned. How dare her? He seized her by the arm and forcefully kissed her. She pushed him away and slapped his face. Then she stood up immediately.

"Have you no shame? No respect for a lady? When I say no, I mean no." she barked at him and started for the door.
Still nurturing his face, he pulled her back and held her neck tightly. It was choking, and she found it hard to breathe.

"You would regret this, I tell you. Consider yourself jobless because I am going to see to the end of you in that company, you slut." He said gruesomely.

She wriggled herself free from his grasp, adjusted her clothes, and scoffed.

"I see you don't like the product. I will take my leave now." She said and left the office successfully this time around.

> **Finally, brethren, whatever things are true, whatever things are noble, whatever things are just, whatever things are pure, whatever things are lovely, whatever things are of good report, if there is any virtue and if there is anything praiseworthy—meditate on these things** - *Phil. 4:8*

It was clear she was going to face this kind of situation for a while, so she already had herself braced up for whatever aftermath that would come with it. The threat of losing her job was something she foresaw, but she wasn't that bothered about it. She would do her job as an employee, and not as a desperate lady running after money.

As she got into her car, her phone rang. It was Cole. She was grateful he called her; it was as if he always knew the right moment to call. They had gotten inseparable somehow; although, she knew her intentions were not pure when they first met, and even when she followed him around. She knew she really liked him. He was the most sincere and trustworthy person she had ever met in her life, and she was grateful he came into her life.

She had told him about her history with the CEO of the company she went to market at, that she knew he was definitely going to want her in bed, but Cole had told her to be strong for Christ and do what is right. She knew that by turning him down, she has taking a bold step because it could indeed be the end of her career; the career she had built over the years in vanity and sin. She was right to have turned him down, and she was not going to let his threat shake her faith.

The job that seemed to be the world to her, that she had done everything within her human strength to keep and build a career out of doesn't look all that important to her now. It was funny when she recalled the times when she would be the one to offer herself as a sacrificial lamb to men, just to sell products and get promoted.

Yes, she wanted that money to prove something she didn't even understand to her mother, but now, her mother was her world. She had nothing to prove to her or to prove to her own self. She was a better person now, and nobody was going to drag her down the mud.

"Hello." Louisa said simply as she answered the call.
"Hey, how did it go?" Cole asked from his end of the line as she answered.
"Where are you?" She asked him, ignoring his question.
"At work. Hey, are you okay?" He asked, worried now.
"I don't think so. Is it okay if I drop by?"
"Yes, sure."
"Okay, see you in a bit." She said, and hung up.

If there was anything she needed the most then, it was someone who would give her words of encouragements and would lead her through the right scriptures. She might think she was fine, but deep down, she knew it was not okay. She drove speedily to his company, fighting back the dirty feelings she got from herself.

> **"But if a wicked man turns from all his sins which he has committed, keeps all My statutes, and does what is lawful and right, he shall surely live; he shall not die. None of the transgressions which he has committed shall be remembered against him; because of the righteousness which he has done, he shall live. Do I have any pleasure at all that the wicked should die?"** says the Lord God, **"and not that he should turn from his ways and live?** - *Ezekiel 18:21-23*

Chapter 9

> "The righteous cry out, and the Lord hears, and delivers them out of all their troubles."
> - *Psalm 34: 17-18*

Cole stretched out, dropped a glass of juice in front of Louisa, and then sat down facing her. She had cried at first when she arrived at his office. Then, she told him what transpired between her and the CEO. He listened carefully to her and was patient while he talked to her, encouraging her with words from the scriptures. He watched her as she took up the glass and emptied the content at one gulp. He concluded that she must have been really shaken.

"I am really sorry for coming to disturb you at this hour that you are busy with work. I should have gone to Veronica, but, you know she has a lot going on with her." She said as he dropped the glass on the table.

Cole smiled. He liked it when she talked; she had melody and rhythm that went with her words.

"It is fine, really. I appreciate that you came to me to talk; I mean it takes guts and courage to open up. Please, whenever you need someone to talk to or someone to listen, come to me. I will be glad to have you." He said and adjusted himself on the chair.

Louisa laughed as she raised her right brow. "What?"
He laughed with her too. He knew his last statement was awkward.

"You know, sometimes I get lost in my own thoughts too, so we can both share thoughts." He said in conscious defense.
She nodded. "I bet you thought I was some sort of Jezebel when we first met; you know, my attempt to seduce you." She said with a tone of embarrassment.
He laughed.
"Not at all. I saw you as a soul that needed Christ. Like there was something deep down in you shouting for help." He replied.
"Really?"
"No, you were no Jezebel, don't think of yourself like that. You were a woman I want to love with all my heart and protect with all of my strength." He said in plain modesty and honesty.

Louisa liked what she heard, but she had to play it cool, so all she could do was stare at him with her eyes strangely wide home.

"Tell me, what did James 1:2 say?" He asked her.

"It says, count it all joy, my brothers, when you meet trials of various kinds." Louisa said boldly.

"That's right. Your encounter with the CEO of that company is just a trial. So do not let it get to you. That's why I want you to do just as Romans 12:12 as instructed. 'Rejoice in hope, be patient in tribulation, be constant in prayer'. So, when things seem like it is out of your own control, take it to God in Prayers. He is a God of possibilities and not a man."

"Thank you." Louisa said, then looked at her wristwatch. "I have to go now. I'll have to report my sales for today to the director of our department and document it. I also don't want to be late for Bible study today, so I have to go and finish it on time." She said, standing up.

"Okay. Take care then." He said and stood up also, walked her out of the company and returned to his previous duty.

From the very first time Louisa walked into his office to market her goods, he had loved her. He was somewhat disappointed when she offered to go to bed with him just to make sales. When he looked at her and examined her, he knew she just needed Christ to know that she was on the wrong path. He was glad that she finally met Christ and had surrendered her all to Him. He was ready to help her in her walk of righteousness. It would not be easy for her, but he saw that strength, that she would make it if properly guided.

As she was still young in her faith in Christ, he wouldn't want anything to make her waiver and lose it, so proposing a relationship to her at this point was not needed.

Cole was just going to stay by her side and watch her grow in God, and when the time was right, he would make known his intentions to her.

Veronica had stayed up all night with Janet, watching their mother sleep; she was worn out and exhausted. Janet had, at a point slept, but Veronica was troubled. She sat with her Bible, constantly checking on her mother.
If this was indeed the end for her mother as the doctors had said, she needed to help her mother accept Christ genuinely. Her mother was a Christian, in fact, she was the one who brought them up in Christ, but they all knew her mother just attended church to keep up with her moral behavior; whereas, Christianity and true righteousness were different from good morals.

Some minutes past five in the morning, her mother woke up and moved her hands to stroke Veronica's hair. Veronica had fallen asleep by her bedside, holding her hands. She prayed that God would soften her mother's heart and allow her to talk to her about Christ.

Veronica woke up immediately she felt her hair being stroked.
 "Mum?" She said, raising her head.

Her mother smiled, it was brighter than the last time.
"Hello, dear." Her voice was weak.
Veronica sniffed, but she was happy. She felt good that she had the opportunity to talk to her mother.

"How are you feeling?" She asked, touching her mother's forehead.
"I'm dying, so I really don't know how to describe that feeling?"
Veronica shook her head, and tears came down.

"Mum, do not talk like that. Do you believe in miracles?" she asked her mother.
Janet stirred on the couch where she slept. They were talking in hushed tones, but they heard themselves.

She took her time to answer. "Well, yes. I think. I don't know, they do talk about miracles in Church. I mean, it is in the Bible. Jesus performed a lot of miracles." Her mother talked slowly.

"Mum, do you believe in Jesus Christ, that He is your Lord and personal savior? Do you believe He came down to earth, leaving His Heavenly possession to die for us, our sins?"
"Veronica."
"Mum, please."
Her mother went silent for a while.
"If I am honest, I have never really had this real conviction of Jesus Christ, and that is why I don't take you seriously when you talk about Him all the time."

> **That was the true Light which gives light to every man coming into the world.** - *John 1:9*

"Mum, you have served in the house of God, but you have not actually lived for Him. It would all be vanity and a waste if you die now and do not have Christ. Every of your dedication to him, going to church on Sundays, attending weekly activities, giving charity, helping the poor, and being a worker for Christ would mean nothing, why? Because your righteousness was never in alignment with the gospel. You have only lived a moral life and not a life in Jesus Christ. You have called the name of Christ, but you do not really know Him. I know that you know all about the death of Jesus, but are you going to let it waste? You understand what it was for and you know why, so why not accept this Jesus. Let him lead you aright, Mummy." Veronica paused and checked if her mother was still with her.

She continued when she saw that her mother was listening quietly and carefully.

"Do you know what 2 Timothy 1:19 says? It says, 'He has saved us and called us to a holy life-not because of anything we have done but because of his own purpose and grace. This grace was given us in Christ Jesus before the beginning of time'. You have received that Grace of God from Christ, why not let Him fulfill His purpose in your life? Let Jesus in, so you can testify of His goodness. Miracles happen, and I want you to believe that, Mum. The story of the paralytic man in the Bible, Matthew 9:1-8. The man was brought by his friends to Christ, he was forgiven of his sins, and at that moment he got instant healing." She looked at her mum, in the dim room, she saw tears rolling down.

"Matthew 9:27-31, two blind men approached Jesus, called Him the son of David, believing he was the Christ, the Messiah, and believing He could heal them, Jesus opened their eyes and made them see. Just because they believed in Jesus Christ, they got their miracles. They repented, honoring Him as Christ, and they turned to God. There is nothing God cannot do; your sickness is minor to Him. With God, all things are possible. Whatever the doctors have said you are feeling, put that aside and trust the Almighty, the author, and finisher of our faith."

She heard her mother wail silently, she held her hands tightly and remained silent to give her mother time for self-reflection. After a while, she continued.

"Mum, why don't you just truly accept Jesus, repent, and lay your life in His hands, so that you can claim what truly belongs to you in the Kingdom? Which is your inheritance as heir to the Kingdom. Are you ready to accept Jesus today? Are you ready to surrender to Him?" Veronica asked confidently.
Her mother sniffed. "Yes, I want Him. I have been so wrong all along."

Veronica was satisfied.
"Then pray with me. Jesus, thank you for your boundless love; for giving yourself for the redemption of our sins. You have shown that God's love for us is immeasurable and has no limits. For this, we are grateful. Lord Jesus, today, I accept you as my Lord and personal savior as I no longer want to live a life of vanity anymore. I ask for your divine miracles in my life today, work in your ways. Thank you, Jesus Christ, Thank you Holy spirit and Thank you, God."

Her mother repeated after her, and they said their Amen.

"Rest now, Mum." Veronica said as her mother slowly closed her eyes. She wiped the tears from her mother's face and went to the second chair in the room. Janet woke up.

"Have you been up all night?" She asked as she stood up.

"Not really." Veronica replied.

"Come sleep here. I will watch after her now." Veronica thanked her and obliged. She could sleep now with no worries. She closed her eyes and said a short prayer of thanksgiving over the repentance of her mother.

> "But those who hope in the Lord,
> He will renew their strength.
> They will soar on wings like eagles;
> they will run and not grow weary,
> they will walk and not be faint."
> -Isaiah 40:31

Louisa got to work a few minutes late, she hurried to her desk, emptied the contents of her bag on the table: her laptop, phone, car keys, and Bible. She looked over her desk to see if Veronica was around, but she wasn't. She felt sorry for Veronica; she knew she must be going through a lot. The day Cole and herself went to see Veronica at the hospital; she had looked so worn out and tired. They had prayed with her and Cole, like his usual self, had given her words of encouragement.

Lillian came bearing the information that Mr. Petkoff wanted to see her. She knew it would be about the issue she had with marketing the products the previous day. She was sure she was in for a handful of words. Without much delay, she went to him, and the aura she got from his expression was not lovely.

"Good morning sir." She said.
He nodded and threw a white envelope on the table.
"I hope you have your brown boxes ready?" he said.
She tried to understand what he said.
"I don't understand you, sir." She said not minding the envelope he threw on the table.
"Pick that up. It is yours."

She picked the envelope, and without looking away from him, she tore it open. She read its content, her hands fell. It happened after all, but she was not going to give up without a fight.

"I've been fired? What did I do to deserve this?"
He laughed.
"Let's just say, you didn't play your cards right this time. How can you raise your filthy hands to slap a CEO, not just any CEO, but the major stakeholder of this company? What were you thinking?"
Louisa scoffed.

"And because of that, you fired me. I have been getting sales for this company all this while without hearing my own side of the story"

"What could that side be? He asked for sex, and you didn't give in?" he laughed. "You have been doing it since, so

what's with the sudden change?"
Louisa felt insulted and dirty. Why did this feeling keep coming back? She swallowed her saliva; it was stuck to her throat, although she used it as a means of holding back her tears.

"It's all vanity." She murmured to herself when she realized how vain and empty everything she had worked for was.

"I'm sorry, I can't hear you."
She bowed her head slightly and left the office. She packed her things in an already provided box on her desk. She walked out of the office without looking back.

Veronica went to Kwame's house to check on him, in order to change the environment from being in the hospital all this while. Although he had talked to her on the phone constantly, she still felt his absence. On getting to his house, she met him cooking. He had a special cabinet for himself, where he could easily reach things without the need to stand up. Veronica laughed at the sight of him in the kitchen.

"What are you doing?" she asked as she helped him with the can of salt he was trying to reach.
"Cooking, what do you think?" he replied her.
She smiled.
"That's great, because I am famished." She said.
"Really? Well, help me set the table." He requested.
She quickly set the table, and when they were done cooking, they settled down to eat, after praying on the food.

"How is your mother doing?" He asked her.
She drank from a glass of water and then dropped it.

"Uhm, Fine. I mean she's still in the same state, but something glorious has happened to her." She smiled.

"Really? Tell me about it." He said, cleaning his mouth with the table napkin.
"Well, I led her to Christ." She said excitedly.

He dropped his fork. "Wow, that is just great and glorious, indeed. Glory to God!"
Veronica nodded. "I know God is good. I now have this kind of rest of mind. I still believe God is going to do wonders and grant her miracle."

"Amen." He added.
They continued their food in silence. When they were through with their lunch, they rested at the porch.

"Veronica." He called her name to have her attention.
She turned to face him, but he almost lost all the confidence and courage he had been building all day long.

"Yes?" she said, smiling.
He took in a deep breath; the worst that could happen was rejection. He started.

"Veronica, you are an amazing, beautiful and God-fearing woman. All along, my life has been empty, and it seemed void, but the moment you stepped back in, you gave me a reason to want to live. You gave me joy and filled me with peace and fulfillment; I don't know how you feel or if you feel the same, but I do love you, and I want you to be a part of my life forever. Believe me when I tell you this Veronica, you are the love of my life. You have been there from the beginning, and till now. You know my faults and wrongdoings, still, you have chosen to be by my side. There is no love greater than that except the love of God, and you love God. I want you to be the mother of my kids too, I want a happy family with you." He stopped and looked at her.

She was utterly speechless; she couldn't believe this was happening to her right now. Her silence was discouraging to Kwame, so he decided to say something. Anything.

"I know it might be selfish of me, considering my state and I understand if you don't want me but…"
"Yes!" she shouted, smiling.

He looked confused; he wasn't sure what her yes was for.
"Yes? Yes, you would-"
"Yes, I will marry you, that is if you are proposing. Are you proposing?" She interrupted, and she felt a flush of embarrassment.

He laughed and put his hands into his pocket, he brought out and opened a pearl-like box, and in it was a three-carat diamond ring. Veronica gasped.

"Veronica Saunders, will you marry me?" He asked, smiling.
She placed her hands over her mouth.
"I mean, I would have knelt down to make it more proper but…"
He laughed, and she joined him.
"Don't be silly. Yes, I will marry you, Kwame. I will." She said and stretched her left hand forward.

He took out the ring and slipped it on her finger. She hugged him.

Finally, this day had come for her. She was now engaged. Veronica laughed at the thought of it. Her mother would be so happy to hear the news. The will of God will always come to be, no matter how long it takes.

> **It is better to trust in the Lord**
> **Than to put confidence in man.**
> - *Psalm 118:8*

Cole offered to take Louisa out to eat something sweet, since she was feeling low about losing her job. It was something she had expected, but it was too sudden. She ordered for another cone of iced cream; taking the ice cream helped her to get lost in her thoughts to the extent that she forgot she had come out with Cole.

"Don't you think you have had enough?" He asked, seizing the spoon she was using to scoop the ice cream. That was the third ice cream for the night.

"I brought you out to take something sweet and feel good, not raise your blood sugar level to its highest point."

She sighed. "I'm just so upset, how can they do that without even considering my contribution to the company? He even had to rub it in my face that I used to sleep with men."

"It is going to be fine. Besides, you can start all over again, this time pure and clean."

"You are right, Cole." She agreed with him. "I should start sending out my CV and applying for jobs."

"That's just the spirit, dear."
As they continued to talk about other things and how great life was going to be, two women spotted Louisa. They knew her and they had been stalking her for a while now, and seeing her with another man made them conclude this was the best time to deal with her.

"Hello, you slutty whore." The woman with blonde hair said.
Cole looked at them.

"Can we help you?" He asked the ladies.
"Ask the slut you are with. Are you married?" The red haired woman asked.
She looked at his hands, no rings.

"No, you are not."
"Excuse me." Louisa said angrily.
"Oh! Shut your whore looking mouth, only God knows where it has been." The blonde responded.

Cole calmed down and tried to weigh the situation patiently.
"Ladies, I think you are mistaken. Now, if you would just leave and lets us be in peace." He said.

The ladies looked at themselves and laughed. It aroused the interest of others and, one by one, they started coming to them.

"This 'lady, hop in my bed' here should be tamed." She turned to Louisa and slapped in her face. "Stop sleeping about with men just to market your products, stop going to my husband, don't go to her man either, don't go to nobody's man selling yourself cheap."

Louisa felt crushed. The people who had gathered around made 'boos' and 'oohs.' Cole tried pushing the ladies away in a gentleman way.

"Don't touch me. I know your woman is somewhere waiting for you to come home but you are here with this cheap slut." The red hair ranted.
"And if she is by chance your woman, man I have to tell you, you've got to chain her down for months, so she won't be getting it from other men." The blonde added.

The blonde looked at the red haired and they pushed their way out of the small crowd that had formed around them. Cole pulled up Louisa, who had buried her face in her hands, and took her to his car. Louisa wept bitterly and uncontrollably. Cole was confused. It all happened too fast.

"Cole, I'm sorry. I'm so sorry, please." She begged amidst her tears, feeling guilty for pulling him into the mud with her. He patted her back as she leaned on his shoulder.

"It is okay. You don't have to be sorry." He comforted her.

She still cried, soaking his white shirt with her tears.

"Even Jesus would be ashamed of me." She blurted out.

"No, no. That's not true. Jesus is your comforter, talk to Him in prayers; He would listen and give you peace. This will all soon pass. Even Jesus was jeered at, so don't think you are alone in this."

Immediately he dropped her at home and left, Louisa wept louder and louder. She felt tired; she thought she couldn't do anymore. She wanted it to stop as she wanted it all gone but just then; the words of Veronica came to mind. Isaiah 41:13 says, "For I am the Lord your God who takes hold of your right hand and says to you, do not fear; I will help you." Louisa, whenever things seem tough and unbearable, God is with you.

Veronica had told her this after one Sunday service, and she didn't really see the use of it then, but she saw the need for now.

Louisa took her Bible and went on her knees to pray. She prayed for hours for the divine strength of God. God did not give up on her, so she was not going to give up on him.

> **Now faith is the substance of things hoped for, the evidence of things not seen.** - *Hebrews 11:1*

Chapter 10

> But whoever listens to me will dwell safely, And will be secure, without fear of evil." - *Proverbs 1:33*

Veronica and Kwame entered her mother's room in the hospital; her sisters were there, including Tom, Maureen's husband. Veronica planned to announce her engagement to Kwame to the family over dinner. She walked in smiling broadly, she felt different, and even though the environment was not a happy one, she still did her best to put up a smiling face and stay cheerful.

"Hey, family." She greeted them as she entered.
While Ann and Janet replied her, Tom and Maureen greeted Kwame.

"How is she doing?" Veronica asked, going to her mother's side. She was fast asleep, Veronica could tell. Veronica noticed the Bible on the table beside her bed, and smiled.

"Stable. The doctors said she might be able to pull it through and have more months to live." Janet replied.
Veronica was happy, she cupped her cheek.

"That is good news." She said excitedly.
The others all looked at her and exchanged looks.

"I bet that is great news." Janet said, pointing to Veronica's finger.

Veronica looked at it, then turned to Kwame, who gave her encouraging smiles.

"Yes, I'm engaged!"
They all shouted and then briefly cautioned themselves, remembering they were in their sick mother's room.

"Congratulations dearest." Maureen said, hugging her.
"Congrats man." Tom shook Kwame's hand.
"Mama would be so proud of you, and I think you have made the right choice." Janet said, looking at Kwame.
They all laughed.

"Yes, judging from the way you two were at each other's tailback in high school. I'm thrilled." Maureen added.
Ann hugged her sister and then Kwame.

"How about having a congratulatory dinner?" Veronica announced.

"Yes." Ann said.

"Totally." Janet added while Maureen nodded.

Just as they were in their happy mood for Veronica, their mother's cardiac monitor machine started beeping faster than usual. The smiles on their face immediately faded.

"Mum!" Ann and Janet screamed.

Tom rushed to his wife and held her tightly. Veronica rushed in with the doctors; they tried to make her stable. The nurses asked that they all leave the room so that the doctors could do their work efficiently.

Maureen and Ann were in tears already, nothing was sadder than this moment for them. One minute they were rejoicing, the other they were in tears. Veronica held unto Kwame tightly, she was depressed and scared, yet, she was convinced that even if her mother were to pass away at that moment, she had Jesus and her name was in the book of life. She silently prayed for the restoration of her mother's health.

For an hour, the doctors were still in there, and what made it more alarming was that more doctors swooped in. Finally, the doctor in charge of their mother came out, and the expression on his face could not be defined by anybody.

"Doctor, what is going on? How is she?"

The Doctor sighed and gave a long look, then shook his head. Ann fell to the ground even before anything was said.

"Doctor, say something." Veronica said boldly, ready for anything.

> **That in the dispensation of the fullness of the times He might gather together in one all things in Christ, both which are in heaven and which are on earth—in Him.** - *Eph. 1:10*

A YEAR LATER

Louisa sat down in the prison visiting area, waiting for her mother to come out. She sat patiently and looked around; the prisoners were all dressed in the same uniform. There were guards at every entrance watching the prisoners and their visitors. The first time she visited her mother was strange and uncomfortable, but after more visits, she got used to the system. Her face lit up as she saw her mother coming to her with a very welcoming smile.

"Hi, Mum." She said simply and quickly set the table for a simple lunch before the visiting time would be over.

"Hello, Louisa. You are looking bright and happier." Her mother said, collecting the stretched fork from Louisa.

"God has been so good to me over the year." Louisa said, smiling.

"Cole is not with you today?" She asked as she looked around.

"No. He is not; he has things to handle in his office." Louisa replied, it had become a custom for Cole and herself to visit her mother every Wednesday, even the prison wardens had gotten used to it.

"How is your firm doing?" Her mother asked as she chunked beef into her mouth.

"Fine. Cole and I have been working on getting you out of here on time, probably before the end of next month." Louisa informed her.
She sighed and dropped her spoon.
"Louisa, you shouldn't bother about that. I'm paying for all my sins. This is my punishment."

Louisa pushed back the hot words that were on her lips.
"I'm engaged." She said simply, but it carried so many unspoken words with it.

Her mother smiled and took notice of her left hand, where the engagement ring stayed, beautiful.
"It is pretty." She said as she touched it.
"I want you to be there for my wedding."
"Louisa, I can't leave until…."
"It was self-defense Mum, and if you didn't go about claiming guilty, you would have been out of here. It has been a year, haven't you paid for your sins enough?" Louisa asked on the verge of tears. Her mother looked sullen. Louisa put her hands in her bag and brought out some pamphlets, she gave it to her mother who collected it slowly. On the very top, it read:

JESUS, THE LAMB OF GOD.
"That is this week's edition. Jesus, the Lamb of God, has taken away our sins. Forgive yourself mother, and forgive those that offended you. You can't keep on hating yourself, as I always say, we are human, and we are bound to make mistakes." Louisa said, looking at her mother.

"Congratulations on your engagement, my daughter. If God wills it, I will be there for your wedding."

Louisa nodded. She looked at her wristwatch and saw that her visiting time was up, and the guards that at every entrance were already giving them notice.

"I have to go now. I'm organizing a talk for the ladies in my firm; I want to see some people about the talk tomorrow."

"Okay, my regards to my soon to be son-in-law."
Louisa gave her a queer look. "I will do well to deliver your message, don't worry. He would make it up to you for not coming today." She packed the table.

"He has been wonderful, I don't mind." Her mother said, assisting her.

Louisa smiled at her mother; they both stood up when she had packed everything, and hugged each other.

"Stay well and trust in God." Louisa said, giving her mother a light pat on the back.

"You too. And thank you for being here for me always. Bye." Her mother replied, looked at her with a faint smile for a while before she began to walk back to the cell that has become her home for about a year now.

Louisa walked into her firm's reception hall; her female employees have gathered already, arranging the place and putting things together for the talk Louisa was going to give them. She felt so proud of herself as she walked in there, this was something she never knew she could achieve; that she never even dreamt of. She smiled as she recalled the story of Joseph in the Bible, who was sold off to a foreign land by his brothers because they were jealous of him. They were oblivious of the fact that they were pushing him to his destiny and it was all for the greater good. Her case was similar; after they had fired her from Evergreen Skincare and Co, it was tough at first, going on and on for months without work, but with the abiding Grace of God and Cole's constant encouragement, she came up with creating her own marketing firm, which had, within the few months of creation, risen to stardom. It was the most sought after marketing firm in the whole of Amsterdam, New York.

Within an hour, there were all seated down and ready for the talk. As Louisa came before them, they applauded her, and she was honored.

"Good afternoon to you all." She said, smiled in acknowledgment, and continued. "Women are strong, women are willful, women are destined to be great too, so when anyone tells you that you can't make it, look them in the eye and ask them, do you know Esther, do you know Ruth, do you know Deborah? These are great women in the Bible; they have done exceedingly well to prove to the world that women are great. What God has given to us is power, our body is His temple, and that is why we do not place it for sale, that is why we do not rubbish ourselves, that is why we give honor to this body more than anything else." She said and paused, encouraged to continue by the rapt attention from her audience.

"I know that as ladies, the marketing field is the toughest of it all. They all want to be paid to purchase our goods, but no! As women of God, mothers of the nation,

we look them in the eye and say, 'my body is not for sale.' Believe when I say this, I am a living testimony to the threats of it, I have once upon a time succumbed to the world and the conformities of men. I have used my body for sale, but what did I get at the end of it all?"
She paused again, then continued.

"Nothing, why? Because all was vanity. 1 Corinthians 6: 19-20 says, 'Do you know that your bodies are temples of the Holy Spirit, who is in you, whom you have received from God? You are not your own; you were bought at a price. Therefore, honor God with your bodies'. Because Jesus, the Lamb of God, has bought us priceless, we are not just anything or anybody, we are somebody with a purpose, and we are somebody with a great mind. We have yet, greater things to achieve, and that is why you do not just jump into the bed of the next man that wants to buy your marketing products."

She mobbed her face, then walked amidst the audience. "It hurts me more anytime I see ladies going out of their own way, their own will to please lustful men for a cheap price. Why not turn to Jesus, who has redeemed us with so much value and priceless effort? The world-renowned author, Joyce Meyers, says: 'Many people feel so pressured by the expectations of others that it causes them to be frustrated, miserable and confused about what they should do'. But there is a way to live a simple, joy-filled, peaceful life, and the key is learning how to be led by the Holy spirits, not the traditions or expectations of man."

She walked back to the stage.
"Here, we do not work by the flesh, when you go marketing and they demand your body, walk away, you

market products and not your body, which is sacred to God. We will always overcome, so don't worry. I will end it here with this Bible verse that says; 'therefore, I urge you, brothers and sisters, in view of God's mercy, to offer your bodies as a living sacrifice, holy and pleasing unto God- this is your true and proper worship. Do not be conformed by the pattern of this world, but be transformed by the renewing of your mind. Then you will be able to test and approve what God's will is- his good, pleasing, and perfect will'. Romans 12:1-2. Thank you."

She ended. They all stood up and applauded her with cheers and shouts. She smiled as she walked away from the stage to her office.

If this is the little she could do to correct the immoral vices in the world, she was ready to go far to preach the gospel, reaching out to teenagers and young minds. She was impressed with herself and thankful to God that her life could see the light that the world has.

Veronica came into her office a few minutes after she entered. "Hey, Louisa." She said and sat down.

They had become more friendly and free with each other as time went by, that Louisa had offered her a place at her firm, but Veronica had refused, saying she wanted to be off the field. Louisa had invited her to the talk, and the presence of Veronica alone was enough encouragement for her to go on and on. While she was speaking, she saw her walked in, but she didn't pay much attention to her so as not to be distracted.

"Thanks for coming to Veronica."

"You are welcome, I mean you were brilliant up there, I was moved, and I'm sure your people would get it right." Veronica rushed her words.

Louisa nodded. "That is just the most important thing; God should make the words embedded in their hearts."

"He will, He is God." Veronica encouraged.

They chatted about other things, and after a while, Veronica stood up to leave.

"Let me walk you to the car." Louisa offered.

"Oh, don't worry. I bet your audience has a lot of questions. I have done enough to steal you away for a while. We will see in church on Sunday, right?" Veronica said, walking to the door.

"Sure, we will." Louisa replied.

They gave each other goodbye smiles and went back to the order of the day.

> **"Who redeems your life from the pit and crowns you with love and compassion, who satisfies your desires with good things so that your youth is renewed like the eagle's."**
> *-Psalm 103:4-5*

Sunday came, and the people of The Lord's Vineyard Church were all in the mood of worship. Cole was sitting at the front pew in the middle row, alongside with Veronica and Kwame. Maureen and her husband, Tom, was also present with their children sitting in between them. Maureen had the last baby, who was barely a year old, John sitting on her laps. Janet and her son, Jake, were seated on the third pew, and beside them was their mother. Their mother had survived cancer even after the doctors had said she wasn't going to make it. She was so sick that she was at the edge of dying. They all looked divine in their Sunday outfits.

The choristers in their ever-glorious purple robes stood up for to minister. Louisa came out holding the microphone in her hands, looking so gracious and blessed in her robe.

"If you have not seen the mercies of God, then you have a whole lot to ask God for. His Love is ever-abiding and steadfast in our lives, and even with all the sins and iniquities we have committed, He still shows us Love. His Love is not limited to anybody, but to all. He is a God that has shown boundless love over and over again with or without you knowing it, and that is why it pays to serve Him." Louisa said, and the congregation applauded and cheered on.

She looked at Cole where he was seated and smiled at him. He winked at her, but she looked away to concentrate more on the congregation. The instruments began to play. After an interlude, Louisa took her cue to start singing.

"It pays to serve Jesus, I speak from my heart,
He'll always be with us if we do our part
There's naught in this wide world can pleasure afford;
There's peace and contentment in serving the Lord.

CHORUS
I LOVE Him far better than in days of yore
I'll serve Him more truly than ever before,
I'll do as He bids me, whatever the cost,
I'll be a true soldier; I'll die at my post.

And oft when I'm tempted to turn from the track think of my Savior, my mind wanders back
To the place where they nailed Him on Calvary's tree
I heard a voice saying, "I suffered for thee."

A place I remember where I was set free,
'Twas where I found pardon a heaven to me.
There Jesus spoke sweetly to my weary soul,
My sins were forgiven, He made my heart whole.

How rich is the blessing the world cannot give,
I'm satisfied fully for Jesus to live;
Though friends may forsake me and trial arise,
I am trusting Jesus; His Love never dies.

There is no one like Jesus can cheer me today.
His Love and His kindness can ne'er fade away,
In winter and summer, in sunshine and rain,
His Love and affection are always the same.

Will you have this blessing that Jesus bestows,
A free full salvation from sin's bitter throes?
O come to the Savior, to Calvary flee,
The fountain is opened, is flowing for thee."

As the congregation joined the choristers to sing the chorus for the last time, Louisa noticed the tears rolling down from her eyes. They were not tears of sadness or pain, but tears of gratitude that she was in Jesus today. Who would have thought that this was where her life was heading to? That Jesus could wash away her sins and make her whole again. She had received grace and love from God, and she was going to put it to use to win souls for the Kingdom of God, because she understood that Jesus has not come to call the righteous, but the sinners to repentance. If after everything, her life can still work out fine and perfect, she saw no reason why anybody should condemn themselves. Instead, they should turn to God, repent and wholly lean on Him, trusting Him for his goodness and mercy.

Prologue

Louisa is the typical lady about town, who was desperate in her career and would do anything to sell her products. She appears to have it all and need no one; not even God. As time went on, it became tough for her as her past escapade came back hunting her. But, one day, the tables turned, and life took a different turn. She needed a lifeline.

Veronica, a committed believer, hasn't been lucky with men and lost interest in searching for one. She is surrounded by a mix of family members, who both loved and seemingly disliked her. She remained undaunted, but silently nursed the ache in her heart. Until one day.
Kwame had his share of gains and pains. He thought it was all over until he was rescued.

Two mothers fought hard, as their lives took different turns, and won.
Meet these five lives, with different needs and different solutions, as they were touched by love.

This story tells of the love of God towards us all, in spite of our past, mistakes, and failures. You will find out the love of God for your life; how much He cares about you, and how He has your life planned out perfectly. The story also teaches forgiveness as a gift from God and an attitude everyone need to incorporate into daily life

Made in the USA
Middletown, DE
21 February 2025

71614473R00095